Five Scalps
The Story of Edward Rose

by
Jerry Alvus Matney

Bloomington, IN Milton Keynes, UK

 authorHOUSE®

AuthorHouse™
1663 Liberty Drive, Suite 200
Bloomington, IN 47403
www.authorhouse.com
Phone: 1-800-839-8640

AuthorHouse™ UK Ltd.
500 Avebury Boulevard
Central Milton Keynes, MK9 2BE
www.authorhouse.co.uk
Phone: 08001974150

First published by AuthorHouse 11/21/2006

ISBN: 978-1-4259-8134-1 (sc)

Library of Congress Control Number: 2006910281

Printed in the United States of America
Bloomington, Indiana

This book is printed on acid-free paper.

Cover illustration by Conrad M Okerwall

Map illustrations by Brent Naughton

Editorial assistance by D. A. Gordon

To contact the author, write to Jerry Matney at:
Alvus II Publishing
17407 N. Goldwater Drive
Surprise, AZ 85374

Five Scalps

The Story of Edward Rose

by
Jerry Alvus Matney

This book is dedicated to the
friends and readers of
Woman War Chief.

Five Scalps

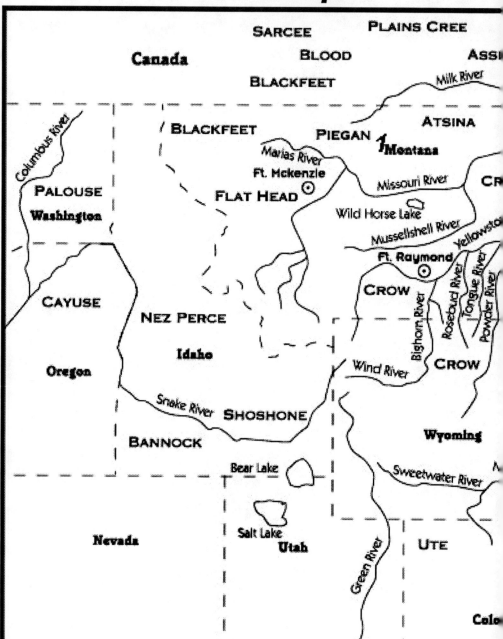

Location Map 1

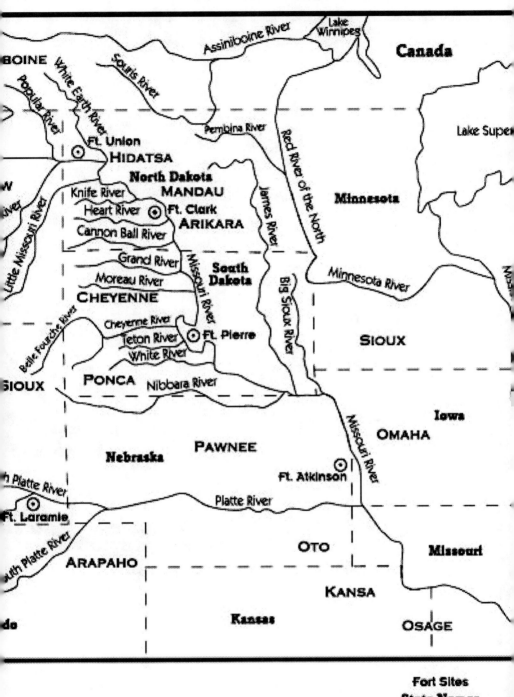

Fort Sites
State Names
NATIVE AMERICAN TRI
River/Lake Names
— — — *State Borders*
Rivers

Five Scalps

Location Map 2

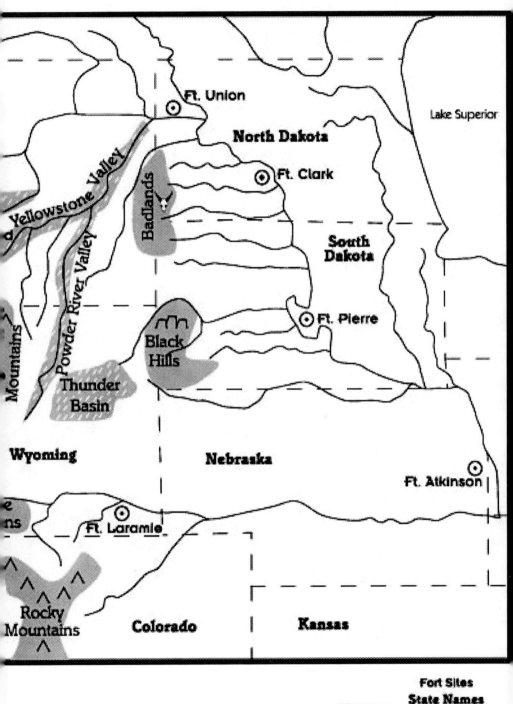

Ft. Union

North Dakota

Lake Superior

Yellowstone Valley

Badlands

Ft. Clark

Powder River Valley

South Dakota

Mountains

Ft. Pierre

Black Hills

Thunder Basin

Wyoming

Nebraska

Ft. Atkinson

ns

Ft. Laramie

Rocky Mountains

Colorado

Kansas

Fort Sites

State Names

∧∧∧ Mountains

Valleys/Grasslands

– – – State Borders

Rivers

Part One

"Five Scalps"

CHAPTER I

After a long day of loading ugly flatboats, Ed's strong back and powerful arms felt weary. All day he had been lifting salted hogsheads, smoked meats, furs, grains and bars of pig iron, all of which was bound for New Orleans. Leaning against a wooden bulkhead, Ed rested for a moment. Soon his mind wandered to thoughts of New Orleans, and his desire to visit the crescent city nestled at the end of the Mississippi. By what he had heard from the boatmen who had been there, the city sounded both wonderful and wicked.

At eighteen, Ed Rose was very much a man. He had matured early in life both from his hard work on the docks and from the physical abuse of his father. Asa Rose, half English and half Cherokee, was a hard-drinking trader who moved his family from the Smokey Mountains of Tennessee to the village of Louisville on the Ohio River. When he was sober, Asa could be successful at trading, but unfortunately, he wasn't sober very often.

Although Ed despised his father Asa, he loved his easy-going mother, who was part Negro and part Cherokee. Although the Rose family was free, many white people still treated them as if they were slaves and not worth much consideration. To help minimize his feelings of rejection, Fatima Rose emphasized her son's Native American heritage.

Ed had learned to accept the fact that his father would occasionally beat him, but Ed refused to accept ill treatment from anyone else. The fire burning in his restless soul cried out for freedom, and the justice he envisioned would come with that freedom.

Only the love Ed felt for his mother kept the young man in Louisville.

Mentally and physically drained, Ed entered The Red Lion, a dark, dingy clapboard building that smelled of cheap whisky and unwashed human bodies. As usual, noisy dockworkers awaiting passage to St. Louis or New Orleans crowded the tavern. From experience, Ed knew that many of these dockworkers would have to work on a flatboat in order to earn a ride down the river.

Ed tried twice to gain the attention of the bartender standing at the other end of the bar, but the man seemed to be ignoring him. Finally, Ed boomed, "Jake, can I have a whisky down here?" Jake stopped talking, nodded to a stranger, and moved toward Ed.

"I've told you before," said Jake, "I ain't gonna serve you whisky because Asa would have my ass for allowin you to get drunk and then be unable to work. But I will get you a beer, just like before." Grabbing a mug, Jake

4

turned to a large barrel. He opened the spigot, filled the glass with foamy brown liquid, and set the mug in front of Ed.

Meanwhile, the short, muscular stranger at the end of the bar left his place and staggered toward Ed. Apparently he was irritated by Ed's interruption.

"*Sacre bleu,*" he belched, "*Monsieur,* do you offer a drink to this *be'be' ne'grillon?* I think it would be against your laws to serve him." Jake ignored the drunk, but Ed understood the Frenchman well enough to know that the man had just insulted him. The stranger not only called him a nigger, but questioned his manhood, right there in front of his waterfront companions. Instantly, Ed became enraged. He charged the Frenchman, who realized too late that he had greatly underestimated this young dark man. Blood flowed from the Frenchman's mouth and left ear lobe. In desperation he counter-attacked by fiercely biting Ed on the forehead. In the meantime, the Frenchman drew a knife from his high-topped boot and cut Ed's nose badly before slashing his cheek.

Ed choked on his own blood as he wrestled the older man for his knife. Violently he bit the man's wrist until the knife dropped to the blood-soaked floor. Though bloody and deeply wounded, Ed beat the Frenchman until the stranger lay in a bloody pile on the dirty floor.

Jake pulled Ed off the lifeless body of the Frenchman and then looked toward two men seated at a nearby table. "Billy," Jake ordered, "you and Able take Rose to Captain Fall's boat and hide him in the cabin. Doctor him as good as you can while I try to stall the sheriff. They'll hang the boy for sure if they catch him. Now move, you hear?"

Billy and Able each grabbed a bloody arm and half-carried, half-dragged Ed to a large keelboat tied to the wharf. There they lit a candle so they could examine their friend's wounds.

Although Ed Rose had cuts on his arms, hands and chest, his face had suffered the greatest injury. On his forehead a jagged circle caused by the Frenchman's teeth bled into Rose's eyes. One nostril had been severed and his cheek had been gashed from the corner of his mouth almost to his ear. Billy and Able covered Ed's wounds with lard and bandaged them with cotton rags. By the time they finished doctoring him, Captain Fall arrived with his boatmen.

Captain Fall examined Ed's wounds himself. He liked the young man and had hired him many times to load his boat. Captain Fall knew that when Ed loaded a boat, the cargo did not shift during passage. Captain Fall nodded at Ed and then dismissed Billy and Able.

Back on the boat deck, Fall yelled, "Stow your gear, lads. We'll cast off as soon as possible. I want to be thirty miles downriver by daylight. I aint turnin this boy over to no damn sheriff for killin a Frenchie, especially not one dumb enough to pick a fight with a dockhand. Now move it!" The men worked quickly to prepare the *Beaver* for sailing. By midnight the boat glided quietly down the river, its box sails catching the stiffening breeze.

During the trip Ed languished below, amid the cargo, waiting for his wounds to heal. Eventually the wounds did heal, but the deep scars would remain with him for life.

CHAPTER 2

At daylight, Captain Fall checked the landmarks on both sides of the river. "Look lively, Jocko," he exhorted. "That is *Otter* Creek on our larboard side. We're makin good time lads, keep her movin." Then Captain Fall entered the cabin to check on Ed Rose again. Although the bleeding had stopped, he could see that the wounds were deep. Because the boy's cuts had not been sutured, the scars would be wide and jagged.

Captain Fall offered Ed some rum cut with water to help replace Ed's body fluids. To numb the pain, he added a small amount of laudanum. The warm liquid soothed Ed's parched throat. As he grew drowsy again, he curled up in the feather-stuffed bedding and fell asleep. Several days passed before Ed became aware of his surroundings.

By the time the *Beaver* reached the mouth of the Tennessee River, the captain allowed Ed to lie on deck so he could observe the river and its shorelines. When they passed a canoe containing natives, Ed's pulse quickened. He had seen Native Americans before but most of them had either adopted white man's ways or had become alcoholic beggars. However, these natives appeared to be healthy hunters and proudly wore their tribal clothing. The boatmen said these were Quapaw, who were known to be friendly to white men.

In the past year, Ed had loaded the *Beaver* many times. The boat was seventy feel long and eighteen feet wide. It was pointed at both the bow and the stern with a large oar amidships for steering. Crewmen walked along each side of the deck using long poles to help propel the boat when there was no wind. The poles created small circular whirlpools as the men pushed them against the river bottom. At the end of each walk, the men pulled their poles from the water and returned to the bow to repeat the cycle.

Ed noticed a change in the color of the water. The starboard side had become dark and cloudy, while the larboard side of the boat remained clear. Captain Fall watched Ed stare into the water. "That is the Mississippi we are joining lad," he said, "and now we are on our way to New Orleans for sure. The muddy water is caused by the Missouri River, which flows all the way from the Rocky Mountains." Ed could not fathom what the Rocky Mountains might be like, but he wanted to visit them too someday.

As the May nights grew more humid, Ed started sleeping on the open deck. The lapping water against the hull and the night sounds of frogs and birds soothed his troubled mind.

Ed missed his mother a lot, but he feared he would be hung if he returned to Louisville. He hardly remembered killing the Frenchman, but he would never forget the pain of the man's sharp knife against his face. He vowed to never allow such a thing to happen to him again. He wanted to become the meanest knife fighter on the river.

One morning Ed noticed Captain Fall sitting on a bale of furs drinking his morning coffee. Ed moved over to sit next to the older man.

"Captain," he queried, "how many times have you been to New Orleans? Are there many Americans down there?" Captain Fall paused to take another sip before he responded.

"I usually sail between Cincinnati and St. Louis. Only since the Treaty of San Lorenzo have Americans been allowed to take their cargo to New Orleans. This is my fifth trip downriver with a legal cargo." He took another sip before continuing. "New Orleans is an international city. The city contains Frenchmen, Englishmen, Portuguese, Creoles, Spaniards, Cajuns, Americans, Cameroons, Quadroons, Mulattos and slaves. Be careful they don't put you on the auction block or place you on a cargo ship bound for China."

Ed's blood rushed to his temples. "I'll kill any sonabitch who tries to capture me," he blurted. "I heard them ships goin to China treat their sailors worse than slaves. At least slaves are valuable because they can be sold. Boatmen don't seem to matter to them folks at all."

Then Ed remembered that he was wanted for murder back in Louisville and he grew quiet.

Guessing what the lad must be thinking, Captain Fall said, "Lad, just be alert and quick of mind and you will learn how to survive. Just be careful, because there are pirates, assassins and thieves all over this river. Trust no one." Ed respected the advice of the older man, so he asked him something he'd had on his mind for a while. "Captain," asked Ed, "how can I learn to fight with knives?"

"If you feel you must fight to survive," replied the Captain, "I can't blame you. Bein black is going to cause you a lot of grief, so I think Jocko can help you. He is the small, wiry Cajun handling the ship's tiller. Don't let his size fool you. He is the best damn man with a knife I've ever seen."

Ed had noticed the small, dark man with the thin mustache. Jocko seldom spoke to other members of the crew and they stayed clear of him. Ed figured Jocko to be about thirty years old.

The captain motioned to Ed to follow him amidships. "Jocko, let me take the tiller for a while. I want you to teach Rose a thing or two about fighting with a knife before we get to New Orleans. He got cut up badly in Louisville and he doesn't want it to happen again." Jocko let go of the helm and walked over to sit by Ed. Jocko looked Ed over. He could tell that the once handsome youth would be scarred for life.

"So, you want to learn how to defend yourself with a knife?" Jocko asked. "I heard you beat that Frenchman with your bare hands. You are lucky I am a Cajun instead of French or I might have to avenge my countryman. My family lives in Barataria, which is below New Orleans. We are hunters, boatmen, guides, fishermen – and sometimes we rob the rich who use our waterway. They are trespassers."

Jocko looked into Ed's piercing black eyes. "The kind of knife you use is not important," he added. "It is more important how you hold and use the knife. Take it gently with your fingers and flick it with your wrist. Keep your balance at all times and hold the knife in front of your body." Jocko demonstrated numerous moves. Ed was mesmerized.

For the next ten days Jocko showed Ed various shapes and sizes of knives, explaining the advantages of each. Jocko was showing Ed some defensive maneuvers when he had to take over the tiller again. Ed practiced by himself, wielding his knife against imaginary assailants.

The boatmen grew excited when the *Beaver* approached a high, rust-colored bluff on the larboard side of the widening river. Wild grapevines, flowering magnolias and large oak trees grew atop the bluff. A motley collection of weatherworn shacks stood below the bluffs, surrounded by numerous keelboats and flatboats. A steep road led up the bluff. Ed learned that this town was called Natchez.

Captain Fall called out, "Jocko, we will not stop at Under the Hill on this trip, so keep the boat in midstream. I want to keep my crew alive and my cargo intact until we reach New Orleans." Ed looked up the bluff as they sailed past the boisterous port town.

Ed often practiced with his knife, and by the time the boat and crew arrived at New Orleans, he felt confident that he could hold his own in a one-on-one knife fight. He told this to his mentor.

"You are ready for any fight, *Monsieur*," said Jocko. "You know how to use a knife, and you are brave and quick. Your scars make you appear older and more experienced than you are. Now, I will give you a name that will place terror in the hearts of your enemies. I name you *'Nez Coupe*, which means 'cut nose'. My friend, be careful in the *Vieux Carre'* because life is cheap and the games are expensive. *Dieu vous be'nisse*—God bless you my friend."

CHAPTER 3

A lively port-of-call, New Orleans anchored ships from all over Europe. The city's taverns and cafes bulged with boisterous drinkers and gamblers, along with numerous ladies of the evening. Ed's eyes took in the sights of the bustling city. Captain Fall had told him that the city burned in 1784, and now the Spanish government was rebuilding the port with brick, stucco, tile and ornamental iron.

The town's sidewalks were constructed of cobblestones, and the streets were paved with a mixture of ground oyster shells, clay and sand. Although New Orleans was Spanish designed and Spanish governed, its heart and spirit remained French. The city's population exceeded six thousand.

Because Ed had only the few coins advanced to him by Captain Fall, he could only watch the excitement around him. He longed to join the revelers. Captain Fall had promised Ed a job working on the docks, and Ed had taken the job. But he knew from experience that the work would be hard and the pay meager.

When winter arrived, traffic on the river slowed to a crawl; fewer ships arrived from the sea. Out of work and wandering through the French Quarter, Ed heard a loud greeting.

"Alloo, *Nez Coupe!* How have you been my friend?" Ed rushed to meet the small Cajun and pumped his hand.

"Jocko!" he exclaimed, "am I glad to see you. I need a job in the worst way. Do you have anything for me?"

Jocko showed Ed a bag of gold coins. "First we play and drink of the juice of life," he said, "then I will take you home with me to Barataria."

Ed and Jocko caroused all night in the *Vieux Carre.* Ed made love for his first time, accompanied by a buxom mulatto gal. By morning they were thoroughly exhausted. Ed slept in the bateau while Jocko paddled them down the Mississippi canal system to Barataria.

When Ed awoke, he found their bateau gliding quietly through salt grass and canes. The cypress trees were covered with Spanish moss, and oak hillocks seemed to rise out of the swamp. Ed noticed many houses built on poles.

Jocko said, "We raise our cemetery and houses because of the high water table and because of hurricanes, which cause heavy rain and high tides." Ed wondered what a hurricane would be like. "We will land here," said Jocko. "That large two story house belongs to my family."

Ed studied the old house. A balcony wrapped around the building on two sides and the home was completely shaded by large trees and vines. Jocko tied the boat to a tree on the levy and led his guest up the path. When they entered the darkened living room, Ed spied a fat old man sitting in a big chair, sipping from a ceramic jug. The man set down his jug and said, *"Soyez be bienvenu.* Will you join me in a *veauverie?"*

Jocko replied, "No, papa, we have just come from *Vieux Carre'* and we still *souffrir."*

The old man laughed and then tipped the jug again. Jocko led Ed into the kitchen. Jocko approached the short, fat woman who stood by the stove, stirring a pot of crayfish gumbo. He hugged her and turned to Ed saying, "Thees ees my *eme'r –* my mother. She will feed us."

Jocko and his mother jabbered in French while Ed watched a young woman plucking feathers from a chicken. A feather protruded from the tip of her pretty nose. Jocko noticed the two young people exchanging glances.

"This is my *soeur*, Juleen," Jocko explained. "Watch out for her, my friend, because she eats men for breakfast." Juleen laughed and then turned back to her work. At eighteen she remained unmarried because her aggressive independence frightened young men away. She liked the looks of her brother's new friend and began to flirt with Ed.

Jocko's mother set out large bowls of gumbo and

black bread for Ed and Jocko. Ed ate hungrily, acutely aware of Juleen's stare.

After they ate, Jocko and Ed retired upstairs. Ed felt as though he had just nodded off when he felt someone fondling him. Ed's eyes opened to see Juleen completely nude and trying to untie his cotton pantaloons. Although he was tired, Ed quickly became aroused. Yet, he was also afraid. Jocko slept on the other side of the dimly lit room. Ed helped Juleen remove his clothes and allowed her to teach him more about the art of lovemaking.

In late afternoon, Jocko awakened Ed, saying, "*Mon ami,* will you sleep all day? For my mother, we must go and hunt. I promised her some fat opossum for her stew, so let's go!"

CHAPTER 4

Over the next few years, Ed and Jocko robbed boatmen up and down the Mississippi. They partied in the *Vieux Carre'* and hung out on the wharves, always looking for new customers to rob. They fenced their stolen goods with various merchants on the New Orleans waterfront.

Physically, Ed grew more powerful and mentally he became more cunning. He feared no one – that is, as long as he had Jocko's blades to back him up. He fought so often that his reputation grew. The name "Ed Rose" brought fear to those who knew of him. When boatmen from St. Louis or Louisville entered New Orleans, they soon learned of the fierce, black man known as *Nez Coupe*. His scars easily identified him to the new arrivals and they wisely kept their distance.

Ed felt people pulling away from him, but that was okay. He only relaxed around Jocko and he stayed close to the village of Barataria. He still had an occasional encounter with Juleen, although he preferred the Cameroons of the *Vieux Carre'*.

On June 6, 1803, the unbelievable happened. Word traveled to New Orleans that the United States had purchased the Louisiana Territory from Napoleon. On November 30th, Spain turned over the ownership of New Orleans to the French. Then on December 20th, France turned the area over to General James Wilkinson, the U. S. Commission, and C. C. Claiborne, the governor of the Mississippi Territory.

Suddenly New Orleans became a world port, open to all trade as a part of the United States of America. Unfortunately, this openness also brought more pirates and members of the underworld to New Orleans. The wide-open city was a long way from the lawmakers of the United States.

In 1806 two brothers arrived in New Orleans and opened a blacksmith shop. Jocko approached Jean Lafitte and his brother Pierre about selling them his booty. Pierre agreed to handle their goods; however, his brother Jean was more interested in smuggling slaves into New Orleans. Pierre had formed an alliance with Dominique You, a rich slave runner who had built a lavish brick mansion on the island of Grand Terre.

Captain You had ships that flew the flags of Cartagena while attacking Spanish ships in the Gulf of Mexico and in the West Indies. He smuggled his slaves and treasures to Barataria where Jean Lafitte set up his headquarters. In turn, Jean fenced the goods in New Orleans through Pierre's business. They sold the slaves on the block from $800 to $1000 each.

As Jocko became more involved with Lafitte and his business ventures, Ed withdrew. He wanted no part of slave trading. He tried to dissuade Jocko, but the man would not give up his newfound wealth. Besides, Jocko argued, this job seemed safer than robbing keelboats. In the meantime, Ed grew tired of Juleen. She now had two of his children and she bothered him constantly about getting married. But Ed did not want a family to interfere with his quest for adventure. At twenty-six, he knew he was in his prime. He needed to leave Barataria and New Orleans.

News came down the river that Captain Lewis and Captain Clark had finally returned from their Corps of Discovery to the Pacific Ocean and back. Ed heard that Lewis and Clark had discovered rich furs in the Rocky Mountains and that they had made peace with the native tribes of the Missouri River system. Ed heard people say that a man could make a fortune in only a few short years of trapping. This prospect appealed to him very much.

Ed bid Jocko and his family adieu. To Jocko he said, "*Mon ami,* thank you for your friendship and your knife skills. My knife has protected me well during our adventures. But now, I must leave Barataria and find my own way. I want to explore the Missouri River and the Rocky Mountains while I'm still young."

Jocko hugged his friend and started to weep. He had grown fond of this wild, black man. Reluctantly, Jocko helped Ed load his pirogue. With misty eyes, he and his sister Juleen watched Ed paddle away until they

19

could no longer see him.

Ed paddled at a steady pace until he reached the docks of New Orleans, where he made one last visit to the *Vieux Carre'* to sleep with his favorite quadroon. At dawn he returned to the docks, where he searched for a keelboat heading to St. Louis. Eventually a boat named *Otter* caught his eye. The large keelboat, about sixty feet long and eighteen feet wide, had a four-foot by four-foot oak rudder and a long oar amidships for steering. The *Otter* reminded him of the *Beaver*.

As Ed stood admiring the boat, a well-dressed French businessman watched him. To Ed, the Frenchman looked prosperous, though he was more muscular than the average businessman. The Frenchman surmised from the onlooker's appearance that he must be the fierce river man, Nez Coupe. He slowly approached Ed.

"*Monsieur*," the Frenchman said, "you admire my boat very much, yes? Do you wish to sign on to St. Louis?"

Ed responded, "*Oui Monsieur,* I wish to enter the beaver trade on the Missouri. Do you have a position for me?"

The man replied, "I am Pierre Menard and, if I am not mistaken, you are called Nez Coupe?"

Ed gave him a rare smile and answered, "I prefer the name Edward Rose. I try to forget my unfortunate scars."

Menard smiled back. "Then I shall call you *Monsieur* Rose. What background do you have for the fur trade, *Monsieur?*"

In his explanation, Ed decided to leave out his life of piracy. He said, "I have trapped all the bayous below New Orleans and I am an excellent hunter. I have shot gators, bears, wildcats and deer, though now they have become scarce on the lower Mississippi. I learned to be a good boatman on the Ohio. I grew up in Louisville." Menard already knew Rose's reputation as a pirate, brawler and knife fighter. Menard also knew the return to St. Louis could be a treacherous voyage because river pirates abounded. It would make good business sense to have a fierce pirate along to protect his cargo of coffee, tobacco and sugar from other pirates.

He replied, *"Monsieur,* I need a good man who can hunt and who can protect my cargo from river thieves. Can you do this job?"

Ed smiled again, "I will keep your larders full of camp meat and no thief will dare attack the *Otter* as long as I am on guard."

"Done," said Menard. "I will pay you fifty dollars in specie when we arrive in St. Louis. We leave tomorrow at daybreak. Good evening."

Ed quickly returned to his stored pirogue. He unloaded his few possessions of linen, cotton clothing, his treasured rifle, long-bladed knives and his French pocket-pistol. He carried his bag of belongings to the *Otter* and stored them in the hold. Then he fell asleep while listening to the creaking planks above him as boatmen finished loading cargo on the *Otter.*

When Ed awoke, he heard the captain yelling for all hands to push off. Then he heard, "Pole! Damn you

21

laggards, pole!" He quickly climbed up to the deck and watched the men lined up on both sides of the deck pushing hand poles into the soft-bottomed river. Slowly the *Otter* moved out of the waterfront and started up the Mississippi.

Ed walked to the stern to seek direction from Menard. "*Monsieur,*" the Frenchman said, "I want you to position yourself here and scan the river for any boats or drift that might be a threat to us. Alert the captain at once so he can maneuver the craft for defense or to evade drifting logs. When we stop to camp, I want you to hunt for deer, bear or turkey to keep our larder filled. We should make about fifteen miles per day with good weather." As directed, Ed diligently scanned the river every day, even though he only spotted a couple of piles of floating driftwood. In the late afternoons he loved to explore the woods and stalk deer or the occasional black bear. Turkeys were elusive in the evening and he had to search for their roosting sites.

After five grueling days, they reached the place called 'Natchez Under the Hill'. Menard and Captain Lambeau personally guarded their cargo while all hands became rip-roaring drunk. The crew brawled, partied and made love until daybreak. Ed roamed and explored the raucous town, but he remained sober.

They laid over one day – for recovery – before again launching the *Otter* in their quest for the port of St. Louis. They polled past the Yazoo and the Arkansas Rivers, and then they finally met the confluence of the great Ohio River. It was difficult to pole their boat past the turbulence created by the junction of the two great rivers. At last, the Mississippi became calm again and travel became easier, but the water ran murkier and they had to navigate more snags and sawyers.

Ed longed for his mother and Louisville, but he knew he could never go home again. He had been gone almost nine years now, and perhaps his mother and father were dead. Although he felt homesick he had a strong desire to see the Missouri and the great Rocky Mountains. He soon turned his melancholy into excitement about his future.

As they ascended the river, traffic became heavier. They met more skiffs, flatboats, dugouts and pirogues. These boats carried supplies, goods or families and their livestock to the new American port of the West – St. Louis. The cargo on these boats included geese, chickens, horses, cows, sheep and pigs, both for personal use and for trade. The boats also carried regular trade goods, such as tin ware, pork, flour, hemp, tobacco, farming tools and whiskey.

A lot of the travelers dressed in linsey-woolsey, made from flax and wool. Some of the men wore loose shirts that reached almost to their knees. These shirts were open in front and overlapped with a belt or tied in back. Some wore large capes across their shoulders. Some of the men wore shirts fashioned from dressed deerskin and breeches made of buckskin, fringed at the seams. Many also wore moccasins instead of cowhide shoes. Most of the women wore plain homespun dresses and handmade scarves.

Occasionally, natives were seen along the river, either staring in wonderment at all the boats or seeking trade from the wealthy white people. The boats also carried Kentuckians, Virginians and Pennsylvanians seeking new adventures or freedom from debts. Some of them traveled west to evade the law.

In the still of the evening Ed could hear the sounds of axes striking wood and the barking of dogs. He loved the smell of wood smoke and frying bacon. Beech, sycamore, willow and cottonwood trees marked the shoreline of the river as they struggled ever onward to their destination. At night, many boats made camp when they could find land high and dry enough to tie up to. Above all, they had to protect their precious cargoes.

As the *Otter* reached St. Genevieve, Ed noticed whitewashed mud walls and many wooden crosses. They saw high bluffs on the western shore and then they came to Carondelet and Cahokia. It had been several weeks since they passed the mouth of the Ohio River. Finally Ed spied the skyline of St. Louis the westward bluffs.

St. Louis was acquired in 1803 with the Louisiana Purchase and the town was just now beginning to grow and prosper. Since Lewis and Clark returned from the Pacific, St. Louis had become a hotbed of excitement for trapping, trading, and the Indian services provided by the federal government.

While waiting for Menard to put his trapping expedition together, Ed walked the streets of St. Louis. The town now numbered over three thousand souls, with new arrivals coming in daily. Most of the houses were built of wood frames, which were daubed with mud, and then whitewashed. Some were built of stone and coated with mortar. A few new stores and homes were even being built with brick.

Ed visited many taverns and bars, listening to trappers and hunters who had returned from the upper Mississippi or the upper Missouri. Not much was known about the upper Missouri. Once again he heard wild tales about giant mountains at the headwaters of the Missouri. However, he also heard tales about fierce native tribes who did not like white men coming into their lands.

CHAPTER 5

While Ed continued his education in the St. Louis taverns, Menard organized a trade expedition for the Missouri River area. He obtained a keelboat and two bateaus, which had come from Canada. These boats were about thirty feet long and eight feet wide. Pointed at both ends, they had flat bottoms and required six oarsmen to operate.

By July Menard had hired twenty-five men including Ed, whom he hired for one season at one hundred dollars American. When the men gathered at the wharf, Menard told them, "Boys, my new trading partner is Mr. Manuel Lisa. He and his family have many years' experience trading on the Mississippi and the Missouri. He knows the Indian tribes with whom we will be dealing and he is friendly with their chiefs. Obey him and show him the same respect you have shown me."

Manuel Lisa was small and dark; he sported a thin, well-manicured mustache. He was quiet and serious, much like Ed himself. However, Lisa seemed unsure of Ed and was not very friendly to him. Ed was not sure he liked Lisa either, but as long as he worked for Menard, Ed would accept Lisa as a condition of employment. In any case, Ed was anxious to be on his way to the Rocky Mountains. He believed that his life to this point had prepared him for this adventure.

The large party left St. Louis and turned up the Missouri River from the wide Mississippi. Ed went ashore on the southwest bank of the Missouri in order to hunt ahead of the boat. As he studied this new countryside, he didn't see much wildlife, though he spotted an occasional domestic cow. At least he was able to kill a few turkeys and one medium-sized black bear for the larder. This country had been well hunted by the ever-growing white population around the village of St. Charles, which he could see across the river to the northeast.

Ed reached the Osage-Woman's River and peered across its mouth, which seemed about thirty yards wide. Then about twenty miles above St. Charles it started to rain. By the time they reached Charrette's, the rain turned to hail and it began to thunder. Ed fired a shot into the air to hail the keelboat. "Hello there!" he yelled. "Bring her ashore. I'm cold and wet as hell out here."

Menard met Rose as the boat came close enough for him to jump aboard. Menard joked, "I see I may have picked a soft hunter. You will have to become stronger to survive among the Osage, *Monsieur*."

Since Ed did not have much of a sense of humor, he simply replied, "When my services are needed, *Mon-*

sieur Menard, I assure you I will make you proud."

During the next week it rained, thundered and hailed most of the time. Their progress slowed appreciably and hunting became limited. They passed the wide Gasconade, the narrow Big Muddy and finally the big Osage River, with a mouth nearly four hundred yards wide. They moved up the Osage River, passing thickly forested areas populated with oak, ash, elm, walnut and hickory trees. When the rain subsided, clouds of mosquitoes flew at the boatmen. Then the sun grew hot and the air became sultry.

Menard and his men were so eagerly greeted at the grand village of the Osage that order had to be restored before trading could begin. As Ed Rose strolled about he noticed men with their heads closely shaved except for a tuft of hair on their crown about two inches high and the size of a person's hand. Many men braided the center of their tuft, allowing it to grow long. Some of them pulled a scalp lock through it and inserted a small bone through the braid to hold the arrangement together. Some men even had silver plates of *Otter* fur decorated with feathers attached to their scalp locks. Menard said that the entire Osage population consisted of six thousand men, women and children.

Ed noted that the Osage warriors were tall, with many of them over six and a half feet in height. A number of the men sported tattoos on their arms, legs or chests. Later Menard explained that those markings denoted war honors or special events in each warrior's life, and that the Osage were very proud of their tattoos.

Ed noticed that most of their bows were made of wood from the *bois d' arc* tree. He recognized a good trade opportunity for obtaining and selling this wood because he had seen none of it around St. Louis, yet it was plentiful in the lower Louisiana Territory. When the head chief appeared for the parley with Menard, Ed and the other boatmen gasped. They had never seen a man as large as this chief. Through an interpreter they learned his name was *Tchong-tas-sab-bee* or 'Black Dog'. He was almost seven feet tall and weighed between two hundred fifty and three hundred pounds. Ed himself was a little over six feet tall with almost two hundred pounds of solid muscle, yet he felt small alongside Black Dog. Ed thought that this chief should be called Big Dog instead of Black Dog.

They also met the chief of the upper village. This chief was called 'Chief White Hair'. However, the interpreter told them that Black Dog was the leader of the entire Osage Nation.

Ed observed Lisa and Menard giving many gifts to the chiefs in order to win their favor. The chiefs in return greatly flattered the white traders. The gift-giving ritual of his employers and the reciprocation in trade impressed Ed. He would remember this the remainder of his trading career.

Ed learned that Osage pipes ranged from bones and stone wrapped in sinew to curved or angled hardwood roots and clay. The pipe bowls were shaped like a disk or were stubby and called a Micmac. Stone bow drills were used to make holes in the pipes, and then they were cured over a fire and smoked until they formed a carbon-caked lining in the bowl. Stone pipes were made of steatite, argillete, shale, limestone, serpentine or a red stone from the Rock River in the North Country. The latter was the most popular and was traded by tribes northeast of Big Sioux Falls.

Eager to get away from the clamor of the village, Ed selected an older native man named 'Turkey Foot' to guide him. Turkey Foot communicated with him by using sign language and a Siouan dialect of the Osage language. Ed learned from his mentor that other tribes linked to this language group included the Mandan, Hidatsa, Crow, Sioux, Assiniboine, Iowa, Oto, Missouri, Omaha, Ponca and Kansa. Ed was good at learning languages and picked up their sounds quickly.

Ed and Turkey Foot hunted and trapped up North Moreau Creek to its headwaters, where they picked up the Lamine River and trapped it down to the Blackwater. When they reached its mouth at the Missouri, they traveled northwest to Arrow Rock and set up a temporary camp to dry their furs and pelts. They waited for the numerous boats of traders and trappers ascending the river to gain transportation back to the main Osage village.

Along the way, they held brief conversations with Launay, La Faysseau, Aird, Captain McClellan, Gravelines, Robidoux and several French Canadian trapping parties.

They were told of a large party behind them that

was coming down the river. Ed waited until he spotted them before firing his rifle and waving to them over the wide river. One of their pirogues with two hunters finally paddled to where he and Turkey Foot stood.

The taller of the men offered, "Hello, thar! I'm George Drouillard and this here is John Potts. We just returned from the whole damned Rocky Mountains. We were with Captain Lewis and Captain Clark and the Corps of Discovery. Boys, we have seen some sights. You boys come on aboard and we will tell you stories you won't believe."

Potts nodded to them as he took their bundles of furs. Ed offered, "I'm Ed Rose and this is Turkey Foot of the Osages. We have been hearin about you fellows for some time now. We heard you boys were on your way back to civilization. How's things up in the mountains?"

Drouillard said, "Son, there is more damn beaver in those streams than you have ever seen. You don't even need traps. All you have to do is sit under a cottonwood tree and wait until they come for tree bark and tender limbs and you just hit them over the head and toss them into your plew bag. We aim to join up with the first crew that will take us back to the Yellowstone."

Ed became excited. He gushed, "I'm with a rich Frenchman by the name a Pierre Menard of New Orleans and a tight-ass Spaniard named Manuel Lisa of St. Louis. I know they'll hire you if you can take us back to the great Osage village down below."

The four paddled out to catch up with the other

boats in the flotilla, where they met up with Peter Wiser, who also wanted to join the Menard and Lisa venture. At Black Dog's village, Ed introduced Drouillard, Wiser and Potts to Menard.

Menard offered, "*Monsieurs,* if you will winter and learn to trap here among the Osage, me and my partner, Manuel Lisa, will pick you up when the ice breaks in the spring."

The men set up camp among the Osage and began to hone their trapping skills. From these men Ed learned everything he could about the Rocky Mountains. He could hardly believe their adventurous tales about crossing over the mountains to the Pacific Ocean and back.

The news excited Ed to the core – this type of adventure was just what he wanted.

CHAPTER 6

On April 19, 1807, Manuel Lisa and Pierre Menard led the St. Louis Missouri Fur Company flotilla up the Missouri River. The flotilla had one large keelboat and four bateaus. The group also carried several dugout canoes for ferrying men and supplies back and forth from the river's banks. Rose, Potts, Wiser and Drouillard had been eager to join the expedition, and Lisa and Menard paid each of them two hundred dollars for joining. Because Ed felt he was worth more than the other men, he simmered about the pay offer.

Lisa's party had been delayed several days because Jean Baptiste Bouche', who had received his pay in advance to care for his family, deserted the party. Bouche' had to be returned to the expedition in chains. Antoine Bissonet also deserted, taking with him several blankets and some camp equipment. Lisa roared at his newly hired trappers.

"Who will go catch that damn thief Bissonet and

bring him back to me? Bring him back dead or alive!"

Drouillard spoke up. "Colonel, if you want his hide, I'll go after it," and with that he grabbed his rifle and took off through the bottoms in a lope. He trailed the renegade Bissonet for hours before spotting the man when he entered a clearing.

"Halt!" called Drouillard. "Damn you! I said, 'Halt'." But the man didn't stop. Tired of chasing Bissonet, Drouillard took a careful bead and fired. After he saw the fugitive fall, he rushed forward. The bleeding deserter screamed at him.

"You have killed me, you bastard! You have killed me for sure!"

Angrily Drouillard answered, "Shut your mouth, you damn thief. You're lucky my shot was off a little or I would have really killed you. When I yell 'halt' you son-of-a-bitch, you had better damn well halt!" Then he half-carried, half-dragged the bleeding man back to Lisa's boat.

"Oh! My God!" Lisa exclaimed. "I did not mean for you to really kill him, *Senor.* I only meant for you to slightly wound him." Lisa sent one of his engages in a dugout to transport the wounded man back to St. Louis.

When the flotilla reached the mouth of the Kansas River, the group met another party comprised of McClellan, Hortiz and Le Compt. Later, Ed learned that Lisa had paid Le Compt five hundred dollars. Although this angered Ed even more, he controlled his urge to quit Lisa because Menard had been very good to him. Perhaps he could still impress Menard so that Menard would tell Lisa to give him a raise.

When the expedition reached the mouth of the wide Platte River, they met a solitary trapper in a canoe loaded with pelts. Lisa led his flotilla to a large sandbar to converse with the stranger. Soon, Drouillard, Wiser and Potts leapt from the keelboat to greet their old comrade from the Corps of Discovery.

Drouillard told Lisa, "Colonel, this is John Colter, the best damn hunter in the West and the toughest man I ever saw. He could whip his weight in Indians. He left us upriver last year to go into the trappin business. I suggest you listen to him and hire him if you can."

Colter told Lisa, "Sir, I have traveled all over the Rockies and most branches of this river and I'm here to tell you that the Yellowstone River country is the best trappin I have ever seen. If you will buy my furs, I'll sign on to lead you to the Bighorn, which has the best beaver in American waters." Lisa relied upon Drouillard, who vouched for Colter, and so he employed Colter on the spot. He assigned the new man to assist Rose in hunting for the party and to serve as a guide to take them to the Bighorn River.

The flotilla continued to work its way up the Missouri, past the Big Sioux, Niobrara, Big White, Bad, Cheyenne, Moreau, Grand and Cannonball, until the party spotted large, earthen, lodge villages surrounded by fields of corn and vegetables. A large sandbar narrowed the Missouri into a swift channel in front of a large village containing sixty round earth lodges. Each lodge had a smokehole at the top. Women, children and old men stood on top of their lodges, waving and yelling at the approaching party.

Wooden pickets and earthen parapets built for defense surrounded the village. These folks had the swift river in front and a large creek protecting them in the back. It was a good place for a village.

Lisa knew these people well. He told his men, "They have three villages with about five hundred warriors and a little over two thousand civilians. I have traded with them many times but they are very suspicious and can be treacherous. They are bitter enemies of the Sioux and Dakota, so never let them see you being friendly with members of those tribes."

Beyond their pickets, Ed could see fields of squash, pumpkins, beans and corn. These people appeared to be farmers rather than buffalo hunters like the other tribes living on the plain. Lisa set up a trade camp on the sandbar in front of the village. While he was trading gunpowder and knives for horses, the Arikara chiefs brought dried squash, cornbread and boiled beans for Lisa's men. Ed enjoyed the Ree food after weeks of eating only salt pork, deer and elk.

As the party moved up from the main village, they saw two additional villages similar to the first, about one half mile from each other. When they reached the Knife River, they came upon the villages of the Mandan and the Hidatsa. In the villages they met some French Canadian traders who had lived among the people in these tribes for several years. One of these traders was Louis Menard, who proceeded to warn Lisa and Pierre Menard.

"Monsieurs," said Louis, "I was robbed of everything two years ago, up on the Yellowstone. There were beavers all over that country, but the Crow think everything belongs to them. They stole all my furs, horses, guns, knives and traps as payment for my trespassing. I advise you to seek permission from their chiefs before you enter Absaroka." An older trader, Toussaint Charbonneau nodded agreement.

"I also have known them many years, *monsieurs,*" said Charbonneau. "I have just returned from the Pacific Ocean. Potts, Wiser, Drouillard and Colter can vouch for me when I tell you the Crow chiefs are most honorable, but their braves and women will steal you blind. The River Crow are under Chief Rotten Belly and the Mountain Crow are under Chief Long Hair. I advise you, *monsieurs*, seek peace with both of them and then place traders among them."

When the flotilla reached the mouth of the Yellowstone, Lisa set up a camp to repair his boats and recheck his supplies. To Pierre he said, "Here, *Senor* Menard, is the perfect location for a future trading post. From this position one can control all the trade on both the upper Missouri and the Yellowstone."

"Oui! Monsieur," replied Pierre. "I agree weeth you, but first we must push on to the Yellowstone and establish ourselves among the Crow."

They worked their way past the Powder, Tongue

and Rosebud Rivers until they reached the mouth of the Bighorn. Pierre called for a landing on the south bank of the Yellowstone above the Bighorn.

"*Monsieur* Lisa," Pierre offered, "I recommend this site for an excellent position to trade with the Crow. If we go further, I fear they will think we are interfering in their trade with the Snakes and Flatheads. They may even suspect us of providing powder and fusils to the Blackfeet."

Lisa had also been studying the country. "I agree, *senor*," he said. "We shall build here. I will name this post 'Fort Ramon' after my eldest son." Despite the name Lisa gave the post, white trappers called it Ft. Raymond or even Ft. Manuel.

CHAPTER 7

Ed hunted during the fall of 1807 while most of the trappers were assigned to build Fort Raymond. They had laid out the post about three hundred feet square with double log stockades. They built a blockhouse on the northeast corner and placed one of the keelboat swivel guns atop to guard the river approach.

Ed roamed up the south side of the Yellowstone bottom until he came to a large stone monolith. The tower was located about a hundred yards from the river. Ed paced over four hundred steps around the rock tower's base. He estimated its height at over two hundred feet. Its walls appeared to be perpendicular except for the northeast corner. Here he located an old trail that led to the top.

Ed could not resist – he had to climb this tower. When he reached the top, he saw that the surface was covered with good topsoil and short grass. The natives had piled two piles of stones on top and had carved pictures of animals and events into the tower walls. On the horizon Ed saw what must be the great Rocky Mountains to the west, and smaller mountains to the south, along the Bighorn River.

As he climbed down the tower, he spied a native sitting atop a horse, watching him. As Ed grew closer, he noticed the warrior had a bow, a quiver of arrows, and a British fusil. Ed was not much worried about the old gun. He worried more that these warriors could fire dozens of accurate arrows, while he could only get off one shot at a time with his black powder rifle.

The stranger eased off his horse and clasped his hands in front of his body with the back of his left hand facing downward. Ed had already learned that this sign meant "peace." Ed returned the same sign back to the man.

As Ed continued his progress down the trail, he hoped the man with him was a Crow and not a Blackfoot, because his life may lay in the balance. The two men cautiously sat down. The native held his left fist in front of him with his flat right hand held just above it. He struck his left palm three times with his thumb and index finger, indicating he wished to smoke and palaver. Ed had learned that everyone was safe as long as the parties agreed to smoke together, for this was the universal peace sign of the plains people.

The stranger extracted a long-stemmed, red-stoned pipe from a beaded pouch and extended it toward Ed. With his left hand, Ed dipped into his possible bag to retrieve a twist of his precious tobacco. He broke off two inches of tobacco twist, took the pipe and pushed the tobacco into the pipe bowl. He then pulled out his strikes-a-light, which was similar to a pistol, but which was used to start fires. He fired the instrument next to a piece of punk in order to start a fire. The native was startled until he saw the smoldering punk. Ed blew on the smoke until a small blaze flared up, then held it to the pipe and drew several times until the tobacco lighted. He blew a long stream of smoke into the air while handing the pipe to the stranger.

The stranger pointed the pipe to the sky, the ground and to the four directions before gently puffing, then he smiled and grunted his approval for the taste of the black man's tobacco. The stranger held his left hand in front of him with the back of it upwards, then rubbed it from his wrist to his fingers back and forth twice. He held his fist above his forehead, palm out and with the other hand pointed to his pompadour hairstyle. Ed understood the man was indicating he was a member of the Crow tribe. He had learned that the Crow called themselves the "Sparrowhawk" people.

This news excited Ed and he retrieved the pipe from the Crow and took four more puffs before returning it. The stranger unslung his fusil and pointed to it while placing his left hand in front of him with his palm down. He took his right hand with his thumb over his fingernails and placed them on top of his left hand, while opening and raising his right hand twice, indicating an explosion. Ed understood the Crow was asking for gunpowder.

The man held his left hand edgewise in front of him

with his thumb up and with his right hand he placed his index and middle finger astride his left hand, pointing first to the horse he was leading and then back to Ed.

Ed understood now that his new friend wanted to exchange his spare horse for some gunpowder. He looked at the gun more closely and saw it was a North West Company trade fusil. Below the pan and on top of the barrel he saw the familiar sitting fox, which faced to its right. Ed had been told that the trade guns were fair for killing game, but not very accurate, especially beyond forty yards. He also knew that the North West and Hudson Bay companies had traded this type of gun since about 1783.

After their smoke, Ed mounted his new spotted pony and led the other man to Fort Raymond. Colter immediately identified the new man as a Crow and signed with him for an hour before relaying the information to Lisa.

"Sir, this Indian is called 'Black Panther'. He's from the River Crow and says his people are gathering their winter meat up in the Powder River valley by followin the main buffalo herds. They'll return to the Little Bighorn to set up winter camp."

Lisa offered presents to Black Panther. To Colter he said, "Tell him to go to his chief and bring the Crow to our fort for the winter. I will offer them many gifts in order to win their trade for robes and furs."

Ed interjected, "*Senor*, why don't you send me with Black Panther so I can begin to learn their language and meet some of their chiefs. Let me take some goods and

I can trade with them during the winter and bring them to the fort when spring returns."

Lisa nodded. "*Senor* Rose, your idea sounds good indeed. I will expect you to return with many robes after the thaw."

Ed left Colter to do the hunting for the brigade, while he and Black Panther led three mules loaded with trade goods down the Yellowstone to explore the new and exciting country that the Crow called Absaroka.

CHAPTER 8

Black Panther guided Ed southeasterly along the Yellowstone until they came to the Rosebud River, then the Tongue River. They ascended the Tongue until they skirted a low mountain range. They traveled east again until they arrived in the Powder River Valley. Just as Black Panther had predicted, they located the tall hourglass-shaped lodges of the River Crow, rested among the cottonwood groves near the river.

Long before they arrived, the travelers could see columns of smoke from jerky being dried and skins being smoked. The camp was a virtual beehive of activity until everyone saw the strange black man being led by the brave warrior, Black Panther.

Black Panther turned to Ed. "The large man is our beloved chief, *Ara-pooh-ash.*" He pointed to the chief's stomach and repeated, 'Rotten Belly'. Black Panther dismounted and told Chief Rotten Belly, "The white men have built a new trading post at the mouth of the Bighorn

River."

Ed untied some of his trade goods in the manner that his mentor, Pierre Menard, had done for the Osage. To impress these people, Ed handed out cloth, vermilion, knives and trade beads. The Crow were pleased and immediately set up a lodge for Ed, offering him women to help him with his lodge. That night Ed thought, "I believe I have finally found my callin." He intended to win these people over if it took everything old Lisa had in his trading post.

Ed settled into Crow life while the weather turned colder and snow flurries arrived in the Powder River Valley. With the buffalo meat dried and the hundreds of bags of pemmican prepared, Rotten Belly directed the River Crow to break camp. They had been lucky on this hunting trip, because they had not encountered any of their enemies, the Cheyenne and the Sioux.

Since they had enough food for the long winter ahead, Rotten Belly announced, "My people, we will winter again at Lodge Grass on the Greasy Grass River. There we will find hay and young, sweet cottonwood for our horses, and firewood to keep our lodges warm. Gather your children and belongings and follow our civil leader Red Bird, who will guide us safely back to Absaroka."

Ed was impressed with how quickly the people prepared to leave. Within two hours, the residents of the Crow camp had their belongings packed on their horses and were ready to move. Little children and women rode astride horses with their personal belongings tied to their saddles. The tribe traveled westerly, back over the route Ed and Black Panther had traced to find the Crow on the Powder River. They crossed the Tongue, then the headwaters of the Rosebud, before reaching the flat valley of the Little Bighorn. The Crow called this area 'Greasy Grass'.

After traveling through the brown hills of the plains, Ed appreciated the green, lush, Little Bighorn River Valley where beaver and *Otter* seemed plentiful. He was pleased to see that the wooded areas along the river sheltered numerous deer and elk, which would provide fresh meat without having to dip into the precious winter food that the Crow held in reserve. Black Panther had told Ed that the harshest time of the winter generally occurred in the last two moons before the big thaw. The air was dry and crisp as Ed pulled his beaver hat down over his ears and tightened his robe over his shivering body as he walked toward the warm lodge.

With Black Panther as a teacher, Ed learned the Crow language rapidly because of his basic knowledge of Osage, which Turkey Foot had taught him. Because these languages evolved from the same language root, they had many similarities.

During the winter Ed learned that his chief was called 'Rotten Belly' because the chief suffered flatulence after every meal. Any large amount of food created severe gas in the chief's intestines. Ed tried to stand upwind from the chief when talking with him.

Ed admired Black Panther and found him to be an excellent shot with either gun or bow. The man was also a great tracker and proved fearless in combat. In December, while hunting at the headwaters of the Tongue, the two men ran into a small hunting party of Cheyenne. Instead of racing away to freedom, Black Panther rode his charger directly into the other party. He fired his fusil only once but before the smoke cleared, he had half-emptied his quiver of arrows at the fleeing Cheyenne. Ed only got off one shot, but the ball found its mark and before the man could get up, Ed leaped upon him, stabbed him, and grabbed his horse. Ed even retrieved all of the man's weapons. He did not realize the significance of his actions until they returned to Lodge Grass.

At the main campfire, Black Panther recounted their adventure to Rotten Belly and the Council. After he told about his own actions, he gestured wildly as he told of his partner's actions.

"My new brother, Black Warrior," he began, "shot a Cheyenne warrior from sixty paces. He charged the enemy, taking away his weapons before he slit the man's throat." Grunts of approval rumbled through the group as Black Panther continued. "He then captured this fine Cheyenne pony, which he wants to present to Ara-pooh-ash, our beloved chief, as a gift for his hospitality. I, Black Panther, attest to Black Warrior's counting of first coup and predict many more acts of bravery for our newest Sparrowhawk warrior."

Chief Rotten Belly, the greatest warrior the Crow Nation had known, rose from his pallet. "Black Warrior," he said, "I accept your gift. I declare you an honored member of the Sparrowhawk Nation and I hereby induct you into the Big Dog Society. You have permission to come calling on my youngest sister, Pretty Woman. I have spoken." Ed beamed at this unexpected tribute. He felt more powerful and more fulfilled than he had ever felt before. The shy eyes of the chief's sister had infatuated him, but he had dared not speak to her until he was allowed to court her openly.

In his excitement, he jumped up and exclaimed, "I have gifts in my lodge for everyone. Come to my tent and receive presents to show my love for my new family. I will call each of you my brother and defend you in battle."

Ed was too giddy to realize that he had given away half of Lisa's trade goods in his first day among the Crow. At the time he did not stop to think that he had not received one robe in return for his precious trade goods. All he could think about was his wonderful feelings, and he determined to never feel second-class again as long as he lived.

After this event, the winter dragged on. Only a few breaks in the weather allowed Ed, Black Panther, Yellow Belly and other hunters to search for deer, elk or sheep. Ed continued to court Pretty Woman and continued to give away Lisa's trade goods so he could stay in the good graces of the Crow people and Chief Rotten Belly.

By the spring thaw, Ed only had enough goods to bribe Rotten Belly to lead his people to the mouth of the Bighorn to trade with Lisa at Fort Raymond. He dreaded returning without beaver and buffalo robes, but he believed his honor and friendship with the Crow would make up for his lack of pelts.

Lisa greeted Chief Rotten Belly with honor and turned to Ed, "*Senor* Rose, where are your goods and where are your pelts? You have been successful, no?"

Ed grimaced as he responded, "*Senor* Lisa, I don't have any pelts but I have spread good will among these people. They think highly of us Americans and they look forward to tradin with us instead of those British limeys. They have given me their word."

Lisa's face turned red. "*Senor!*" he screamed. "I have waited here for you with my boats to load your pelts and you tell me you have nothing! I have lost thousands of dollars in goods and you have nothing to show me. You are a stupido, a pendejo, *senor*. I fire you now so you can stay with your new Crow friends. You no longer work for the Missouri Fur Company. This is what I get for hiring and trusting a nigger." All through the winter, Ed had felt important, had been treated with honor and had even courted the chief's own sister. Now, besides being fired, he was called the foulest name he had been called since he killed that Frenchman in Louisville.

Ed flew into a rage and began pounding Lisa, venting the anger he had acquired from the real and imagined slights since his youth. While Ed punched, kicked and bit Lisa, John Potts tried to restrain him, but Ed was so strong Potts could barely free Lisa, who fled from the fur post and leapt aboard his waiting keelboat.

Lisa yelled, "Flee this mad man! Quickly, get me out of here, you fools!"

While the keelboat sailed down the Yellowstone, Ed

ran to the swivel canon on the blockhouse and fired it at Lisa's boat, narrowly missing one of the men standing in front of the gun. Luckily for Lisa, Ed had not taken the time to aim. By the time the smoke cleared, Lisa was out of range, still screaming at his men to put up more sail and pole faster.

Ed slowly brought his anger under control and sat down on a keg, still watching the keelboat sail downriver. What would he do now? He had no job and no one would employ him after Lisa put out the word that he was a mad man and a thief.

He had felt secure while he was among the Crow because they respected and admired him. His only choice now was to remain with the native people who had adopted him. Perhaps he could become important by controlling the Yellowstone trade with the Crow.

Ed left Fort Raymond and returned with the River Crow to begin his new life among them.

CHAPTER 9

In the spring of 1808, Rotten Belly led the River Crow on the spring hunt. This first hunt of the year was always very important. By spring, the Crow needed to refill their larders and fatten their shrunken bellies. Ed proved to be an excellent hunter and a daring buffalo chaser. He thrilled as he rode into a herd seeking a plump fat cow to bring down; danger made him feel alive. Black Panther and the rest of the hunters were impressed with their new friend's performance. With good success, the River Crow hunted from the mouth of the Pumpkin River to the mouth of the Tongue.

While returning up the Yellowstone River, Black Panther announced, "I wish to hunt the Big Porcupine Creek. Who will follow me?"

Ed responded, "I will follow you my brother. Are there others among you brave enough to follow us?"

Young Yellow Belly grunted and led several of his Hammer Owner members to join the hunt. By the time they crossed the Yellowstone, the party consisted of almost fifty men, many of them young and untried in battle. As Ed looked around, he wished they had more veteran warriors among them. However, at this time of the year, everyone needed meat, so perhaps they would not run into enemy tribes.

Since Ed had never been in this country, he took the opportunity to learn the geography of the new land. Traveling north in the hills above the creek, he noticed that the land became drier and the timber thinner the further they traveled. The group tried to stay along the edge of the valley to avoid detection.

Several miles up the creek they heard sporadic gunfire and immediately pulled into a group of cottonwoods. Quietly, Black Panther rode up the stream to scout the source of the noise. Ed waited with the remainder of the young hunters to keep them in check.

Nearly an hour passed before they heard a horse racing downstream at a full gallop. Ed told his men to get ready, while making sure they kept themselves and their horses concealed in the brush. As they cautiously peered out through the limbs, they saw Black Panther racing directly toward their hiding place. As Black Panther pulled his horse to a halt, he yelled, "Big Bellies! Make ready your weapons. We outnumber these devils. Now we must teach them to stay out of Absaroka. Follow me." Ed felt uncomfortable attacking a party of Hidatsa with this group of untried young men, but he could not allow himself to appear a coward.

"We are with you Black Panther," they yelled. "Lead

us forward. We will show these heathens they cannot poach Sparrowhawk game."

The young men grunted agreement. Almost in unison they yelled, "We are with you brave Black Panther. We will follow you into battle."

It was hard for Black Panther and Ed to keep the nervous and excited young men from blowing their element of surprise. However, the hunters eventually calmed down and quietly approached the bend of the creek. The Hidatsa had trapped a small herd of buffalo near the bluffs and were charging after them with their bows because only a few of the hunters had fusils and none of them had rifles.

When they were within three hundred paces, Black Panther gave the signal to charge. Ed rode just behind his adopted brother. With his rifle raised to his shoulder, he stood straight up in his stirrups, allowing his horse to run at its own pace. He fired one shot for effect at one hundred yards and a Hidatsa warrior fell from his horse. Those who had fusils fired them, and then everyone began firing their bows. Ed reloaded as his horse raced onward and again he dropped one of the enemy hunters. The Crow were almost upon the Hidatsa now and were firing at point blank range with killing effect.

The remaining five intruders raced out of the valley and up onto the bare hills beyond. From there they raced into a rock fortress upon the crest of a hill and laid down a fusillade of fire that stopped the young Crow cold. The Crow immediately sought shelter for themselves about three hundred paces from the rock fort.

Because of his wounded leg, Black Panther de-ferred to Ed to lead a charge upon the enemy fortification. Ed called out, "Who will follow me? Who among you will be brave enough to take the scalps of these Big Bellies?" None of the young men volunteered to follow him. They were young and inexperienced, and they did not know how brave Black Warrior was. They had lost a great deal of their enthusiasm due to the wounding of several of their members, including their leader, Black Panther. No one wanted to leave the safety of his cover.

Ed was not only disgusted by their lack of bravery, but he took their reluctance to follow him as a personal affront. He yelled, "You are women. You are buffalo guts. You have no relatives. I will wipe out these cowards by myself."

With his ego on the line, Ed raced across the hill in a zigzag line, clinging to the neck of his horse. As he neared the fort he pulled out his large butcher knife and leaped headfirst into the midst of the Hidatsa.

The enemy refused to fire until they could figure out what this crazy black Crow was going to do. Now that he was among them, they began to lose hope of quickly disposing of him. They tried to concentrate on the siege they were under, but they had no idea what they were up against.

Ed had been a knife fighter all his adult life and he had learned a great deal from his Cajun friend, Jocko. Grasping his knife with his extended fingers, he began to charge and slash at the alarmed Hidatsa. Although they also had knives, war clubs and spears, they were not as skilled in hand-to-hand combat as their attacker, while Ed was a master.

In less than three minutes, Ed had killed all five of the enemy and had taken their scalps and weapons. He then climbed atop one of the rocks and yelled to his companions, "It is safe to come out now brave ones. I, Black Warrior, have saved you."

In disbelief the young Crow and Black Panther rode to the rock fortress, where they observed the carnage. The nearby rocks were actually slick and red with the blood of slain warriors. Excited, the young men began to yell and chant, and then they began slapping Ed on his back and praising his bravery.

When the party rejoined the River Crow at Horses Creek, Black Panther called together Rotten Belly and the Council. He recounted their battle with the Hidatsa and then told of Black Warrior's charge into the rock fortress. When he finished, everyone grunted their approval and congratulated Ed. Although Ed was actually embarrassed by the accolades given him, he felt great. When things calmed down, Chief Rotten Belly arose. Everyone quieted while waiting to hear what the leader would say about this great event.

"My people," the chief began, "from this day forward, this shall be known as 'The Great Battle of the Rock Fort' and Black Warrior shall forever be known as 'Five Scalps' to memorialize the event. My son, I now proclaim you 'Five Scalps'. Further, I give permission for my sister, Pretty Woman, to join the lodge of our beloved Five Scalps. I, Rotten Belly, state it is so."

The village cheered and whistled their concurrence. Ed would now be a Crow warrior for life. He would be remembered forever in the oral history of the Sparrowhawk people.

The black man rose from his blanket and said, "Chief, I am pleased to give you my best rifle with ball and powder in exchange for Pretty Woman. I will always feed and protect her."

Ed never had to ask for followers again and anytime he was ready to go on a hunt or a horse raid, he had more followers than he really wanted. The bravest of the Big Dogs were now eager to follow his lead. When Black Panther was well, he too was ready for his brother, Five Scalps, to lead him into a battle.

CHAPTER 10

While Ed courted Pretty Woman, he also took on the training of Yellow Belly, the youngest brother of Chief Rotten Belly. Because Ed no longer had any trade goods to make him popular, he had to win over the Crow by being a great hunter, horse thief or warrior. He could also win favor with the chief by making the man's brother, Yellow Belly, a successful warrior and hunter.

He taught Yellow Belly to shoot faster and with more accuracy than most of the Crow, who still relied heavily upon their bows. Ed explained to Yellow Belly that as guns became better and more numerous, the Crow must become more knowledgeable and proficient than the Blackfeet, Cheyenne and Sioux if they were to survive. Even though Yellow Belly was young, sullen, belligerent and withdrawn, nevertheless he was fast, strong and utterly fearless. Ed drew upon these strengths to turn the young man into a fine warrior.

During the brown-grass season of 1808, the River

Crow followed the buffalo herds farther down the Elk River toward its mouth. Ed and Pretty Woman took in Owl Woman to assist them with lodge chores. Successful hunters brought home hides and furs, which needed to be tanned. Also meat had to be dried and jerked. Ed wanted to use the surplus food and hides for trading. Ed also accumulated over one hundred horses from his raids. When he was ready to trade the horses, he approached Chief Rotten Belly.

"My Chief," Ed offered, "I desire to take my horses and hides downriver to trade among the earth lodge people. I will return next thaw." He took his wives and drove his horses and seven loaded packhorses down the Missouri until they reached the large earth lodges of the Minitari. This tribe, also called the Hidatsa, lived near the mouth of the Knife River.

Ed was greeted by *Le Borgne*, the giant, one-eyed Hidatsa chief, who was as fearsome looking as Ed, but much larger. Learning of Ed's desire to trade, *Le Borgne* said, "We too have many horses which we trade to our neighbors, the Mandan. I suggest you take your herd downstream to the Arikara. They are always in need of ponies to trade to the white trappers who come to the mountains. However, I caution you to be careful of Grey Eyes, their principal chief because he is usually angry and quite unpredictable."

Ed thanked the tall, one-eyed chief and then continued on down the Missouri. As he descended below the mouth of the Moreau River, he saw the first of three earth lodge villages of the Arikara, which the white men often called 'Rees'. Ed drove his horses onto a long sandbar opposite the first village and set up a temporary corral to keep them on the bar. Soon several men from the village crossed the narrow channel in buffalo hide bullboats. Their leader recognized the muscular black man with the ugly scar on his forehead. He spoke to Ed fluently in the language of the Crow.

"I am Chief Little Soldier. I remember you when you were here with the white trader, Manuel Lisa. Why are you dressed as a Crow?"

Ed replied in his best Crow. "I am *Chee-ho-carte,* a war chief of the Crow." He held up his arrow quiver decorated with ermine and beadwork. His arrows had been made by the finest arrow-maker in the Crow Nation, which befitted a war chief of high stature. Ed continued, "I am here to meet white men who are coming up the river. I hope to sell some of my horses and beaver plews. For your hospitality, I will share some of my good fortune from my trades."

Little Soldier took Ed's hand. "Welcome to my village," he said. "You may partake of my protection and hospitality."

PART TWO

"Edward Rose"

CHAPTER 11

Ed learned to respect the life of the Arikara but he could see that sooner or later there would be a direct conflict with the other 'Americans'. These white men felt they owned the land all the way to the Pacific Ocean, now that Lewis and Clark had opened the way over the Rocky Mountains.

Ed lived mainly in the village of Little Soldier and tried to stay clear of Chief Grey Eyes in the southern village. Grey Eyes was unpredictable and seemed to hate all Americans, whether black or white. Ed quickly picked up the language of the Arikara, since it was similar to the language of the Crow. He made himself popular with the hunters of the tribe by showing his skill with his Hawken rifle. He even attended a horse raid by the Arikara against the nearby Sioux tribe. The Sioux and Arikara tribes continually raided each other's horses. Ed figured that some horses changed ownership back and forth several times a year.

Ed waited several weeks, carousing with Ree maidens while he waited to trade his goods to a passing trader. He even joined the young people and their elders who sat atop the large earthen domes of their village. He could see for miles down the crooked Missouri River. As he gazed, he viewed a mirage of boats. He covered his eyes and then slowly looked again before realizing that indeed a trading party was ascending the river.

The young people saw the white men first and began to chatter and yell excitedly until the elders also saw the flotilla. When they came into focus, Ed could see there were two keelboats and several smaller craft, all loaded with men and goods. He left the roof of the lodge and ran for his robes and furs, checking on his horses in the corral. When all was ready, he made his way to the riverbank to welcome the visitors from St. Louis.

Ed hailed the lead boat. "Hello there! I'm Ed Rose, a free trapper. Who is your brigade leader and where can I find him?"

A reply came, "We represent *Senor* Manuel Lisa and the Missouri River Trading Company. Our leader and a senior partner is Captain Andrew Henry. Come aboard." Ed waited until the boat was secured to the bank, then he boarded the lead craft. Ed remembered Captain Henry when he led the brigade to build Fort Raymond. Ed held great respect for Henry, so he greeted him warmly.

"Captain, it's great to see you again. Are you willin to trade with me or has Lisa put out the word that I ain't to be trusted?"

Henry shook Ed's hand and said, "Rose, I don't

wish to get involved in your disagreement with *Senor* Lisa. He is my partner but I am in charge of this trading party and I will trade with you if you have the goods. You have proven to be a good hunter and a brave employee. After we set up camp, I will send for you and we can see what you have."

Ed was delighted. "Captain," he said, "you are a true gentleman and I will be proud to trade with you. I promise you the best robes and furs this side of the Rockies. I obtained them myself along the Bighorn River in the heart of Crow country. Your boys at Fort Raymond could not get anything better."

Ed paid several young men to carry his goods and lead his horses toward the white men's camp. He was walking around, talking to some of his old acquaintances, when he spotted an old friend from his trip up the river from St. Louis.

"Glass, is that you?" he asked. "I'll be damned if it ain't old Hugh Glass. You old pirate, are you still alive? I thought you had gone under by now and yet here you are, just as ugly as ever."

Glass grabbed Ed's hand. "You're the pirate, Rose," he said. "I was just Lafitte's slave, but you were tradin with those French crooks. I remember you and that thief, Jocko, when you two would rob anyone who entered Baratarria." Ed almost blushed. He knew Hugh was teasing him, but the truth of his words wounded his pride; he did not want others in the camp to know that he once was a thief and a pirate. He led Glass away from the camp so they could talk in private.

"I have done well by the Crow," he said. "I learned their language and became a war chief among them. They are good people when you get to know them. They will steal you blind, but they are loyal to their friends and will fight to the death to defend your life or your honor. I consider Chief Long Hair and Chief Rotten Belly to be two of the finest people I have ever known."

Hugh nodded. "Well Rose, I knew you would do well among those savages because they respect good hunters and fighters. I did pretty well among the Osage, but I had to get back among white people because I am too old to change my ways. Maybe if you could set me up good with the Crow, I could stay in the mountains instead of always bein broke in St. Louis."

They were just getting into details when a young boatman approached. "Rose," he said to Ed, "Captain Henry will see you in his camp now. He is over yonder by the grove of cottonwood trees." Ed called to his young braves, asking them to bring his horses and goods to Henry's campfire.

"Rose," Henry began, "I am willing to buy all of your furs at the market price in St. Louis. I also will buy all your horses, provided you will agree to work for me again. I need your contacts among the Crow and your ability to interpret among the other tribes along the Missouri. I will place your credit in our records in St. Louis and you can draw on your account any time you want with any representative of our firm. Are you agreeable?"

Ed shook Henry's hand firmly. "I am pleased to work for you again Major," he said, "and I only ask that if any complaints are ever made toward me that I be allowed to address those charges in front of you personally."

Henry responded, "I agree totally. Now, I want you to meet Rueben Lewis, the brother of Governor Meriwether Lewis. He is one of my newest junior partners. I want you to take him to the Crow and see how many furs you can trade from them. I'm going to take the rest of my brigade up to the Three Forks and do some serious trapping. I have given Rueben seven thousand dollars in trade goods, but I have asked him to use the lot frugally."

Lewis interjected, "Major, Rose and I will get along just fine. You don't need to worry about us. We'll see you in the spring with lots of beaver." Ed was ecstatic. He was now back in the thick of the mountain fur trade and once again he felt important. He made a promise to himself to not let Major Henry down and to protect Lewis with his very life. When they reached the Bighorn Hot Springs, they found the entire Crow Nation.

Ed called out, "My friends, we bring you gifts. Bring your furs to us and we will reward you handsomely. Tell all your bands to bring in their trade items." Lewis was surprised by Ed's method, but he still had confidence in him, and he noticed how popular Ed was among the Crow. He dared not try to stop him from giving away their goods.

As the days passed, there were no goods left and Ed had received very few furs. Lewis was disgusted and ready to make charges against Ed. While he was deciding his course of action, Moses Carson appeared at the

Crow camp.

"Captain Lewis," he stammered, "I've got bad news for you, sir. I have been sent here by Captain William Clark, who said to tell you that Meriwether has been killed over on the Natchez Trace."

Rueben was devastated by the news because his older brother had been his idol. He knew Meriwether was having trouble administering the large Louisiana Territory and that he was having problems with his financial records. He had promised to take all his books and receipts to Washington to clear up any claims of impropriety. Rueben could not believe his brother was dead at only thirty-five years of age. Who would want to kill Meriwether Lewis anyway?

Carson did not have the heart to tell Rueben that the early reports were that Meriwether may have committed suicide. He had also heard that Lewis was getting more unstable and mixed up. His affairs became more confusing for him as the pressures of his responsibilities as the governor of the Louisiana Territory increased. Rueben packed what few supplies he had left and the furs from Ed's limited trading and headed toward St. Louis with Carson.

After the trading party left, Ed breathed a sigh of relief. He knew he had been too generous with the Missouri Fur Company goods, but this had made him very popular among the Crow again. Ed stayed on the sand bar until a French trader rode into camp with two pack-horses loaded with trade goods. Ed's eyes lit up when he recognized his old friend, Toussaint Charbonneau.

"Hey there, Charbonneau," he called. "What the hell are you doin in these parts? I thought you loved them Minitaris. I'm surprised they haven't hung you for cheatin them or stealin their young girls."

"*Monsieur Nez Coupe',*" Charbonneau replied, "how are you among the Crow? Did you get many furs? Have you chased their women from their villages yet?"

Ed laughed. "You old faker, you're the one who buys all the young squaws for yourself. I don't stand a chance with you in the mountains."

Charbonneau offered, "Come with me, *Monsieur,* and we can earn riches in the trade of young maidens. I am going to the Snake River Shoshoni to buy captive Arapaho girls. I will trade them to the fur trappers to keep them warm during the winter. They will reward me with many furs, which I will trade to *Senor* Lisa and Captain Henry."

Ed said, "Well, I'll be damned. How about if I pick out a good one for myself? By the way, where is that pretty wife of yours?"

"Oh, she is with child again. I left her at Fort Lisa on the Missouri River because she is too much of a burden to me and my trade."

Ed had met Sacagawea and could not imagine why Charbonneau would leave her at a fur post among mountain men who had not been with a woman for months. He did not think he could be trusted to be too close to her himself. She was something special. However, he was thrilled to have something to occupy his nervous energy because he was bored just sitting around the camp day after day.

They traveled along together. When they reached the Shoshoni, near the headwaters of the Snake River, Ed found out that the Shoshoni did indeed have several Arapaho maidens. Charbonneau traded for ten of them while Ed bargained with several Shoshoni braves. Charbonneau was shocked when he saw Ed trade his rifle, lead and powder for a single bow and a quiver full of arrows. Charbonneau had counted on Ed's marksmanship to protect him from the Blackfeet and now he was practically defenseless.

Charbonneau cried out, "*Monsieur* Rose, you have given away all your weapons. How will we defend ourselves from our enemies?"

Ed laughed and quipped, "A real man only needs to use his mind and not rely upon guns and powder. Stay with me and I will defend you old friend." Charbonneau began to fear for his life as he followed Ed and the female captives. The women were worth a great deal in money to the mountain men, but Charbonneau considered his life was worth much more. He was sure that his crazy friend would get them all killed and he trembled with fear.

When they reached the Seedskadee (Prairie Hen) River, which the trappers also called the Green River, they met another party of Shoshoni. To Toussaint's horror, Ed gave away his bow and arrows without getting anything in return. Charbonneau had no weapons because he had depended solely upon Edward Rose for protection. He became alarmed.

"*Monsieur*," he exclaimed, "why do you do this perfidy? Have you a death wish for your old *ami*?" Ed decided to really frighten his old friend and test his mettle even more. He saw a Shoshoni on a ridge and beckoned to him in sign language to come to him to trade. They sat around the campfire while negotiating and smoking for some time. Then Ed gave his pipe and his knife to the Shoshoni brave while Charbonneau shook with terror.

"*Monsieur*," he cried, "surely we will starve and our enemies will scalp our emaciated bodies."

Ed frowned. "The man who can't live in this country full a game, even without arms, deserves to die." He took Toussaint's knife and broke off the blade, while Charbonneau began to softly cry. If Charbonneau had not been so afraid of Rose, he would have attacked him with a club.

Instead Charbonneau whined, "What will we do, *Monsieur* Rose? What will we do?"

Ed laughed, "You old fool! We can live on grasshoppers like the Digger Indians."

Then Ed suddenly abandoned Charbonneau and his girls and entered a willow thicket. When he returned he had a spear made from the broken blade of Charbonneau's knife. When they reached a buffalo herd, Ed sneaked in among the animals and speared an old bull. He directed the maidens to strip the meat from the carcass and dry it for travel food.

Charbonneau calmed down. He ate his fill of tongue, liver and intestines. He was at ease now and was slowly forgiving Ed for terrifying him. However, he would never feel safe until he returned to Metaharta.

After a month of travel they finally reached the villages of the Minitari (Hidatsa) on the Heart River. Ed had traded one of the maidens for a porcupine-hunting shirt, leggings, belt and long hair with some gum to stick it to his own. He was a real dandy indeed. However, just as they were becoming popular in the village, one of the young warriors recognized Ed for having killed one of his comrades at the Rock Fort fight on the plains.

Before the Hidatsa could organize revenge, Ed quickly traded for a canoe and fled from the village. Charbonneau, fearing for his life, fled with Rose. In his rush to escape, Toussaint almost swamped their boat.

They paddled down river for five days until they reached safety among the Arikara. Chief Little Soldier was so delighted to see Ed that he gave him a large white stallion. Ed was pleased since he had hurriedly left his mounts up river in Metaharta. Ed took great pride in his new steed and paraded it around the villages. This irritated Chief Grey Eyes. He did not like this black intruder and encouraged his braves to avoid going on hunts or raids with him. Someday he promised himself he would see the man called 'Five Scalps' disgraced among his people. He was jealous of the attention given Ed.

During midsummer, a Yankton Sioux party entered the village to trade. One large buck became offended by Ed's newly acquired apparel and in sign language began to poke fun at Ed's appearance. He ridiculed him for trying to appear as a Hidatsa warrior in his finery. While

Ed was talking to Little Soldier, the Sioux brave tied a deer's foot to his war club and made a challenge toward Ed.

Ed drew his Green River knife to attack the Sioux, but some of the Arikara warriors restrained him before he could inflict any harm to the guest. When peace was restored, the Sioux party moved on down the river.

Ed again gained attention among the Arikara by painting vermillion handprints on his new white horse. He also placed red handprints fore and aft on his new hunting shirt. He even painted one half of his face red and the other side black. However, as the months passed, Ed again grew restless, and at last he headed back toward Absaroka to find his Crow family. He located the main village at the Bighorn hot springs on the Bighorn River. Here Ed settled down for a while.

When the first winter storms rolled in, Chief Rotten Belly moved the River Crow down river to the mouth of the Greybull. Chief Long Hair moved his Mountain Crow up the river to the mouth of the Popo Agie, where it empties into the Wind River.

From the Grey Bull, Ed spent a great deal of time with some of his young Crow hunters in the Shell Canyon area. Trees were plentiful and the hunting was good. He enjoyed the peaceful feeling of the area and considered it the most beautiful location in Absaroka.

CHAPTER 12

As usual, Ed once again became bored with lodge life. He called the young men together. "My young warriors, I have decided to cross over Medicine Wheel Pass and hunt buffalo in the area of the Tongue River. Who will ride with me?"

Always eager to follow their idol, they began to whoop, *"Ka'he! Ka'he!"* Ed led them around Horseshoe Mountain to the headwaters of the Tongue River, where they followed the old buffalo trace to the junction of the Little Tongue. Here they ran headlong into a white trapping party.

Ed called, "Halloo there! We are friendly Crow hunters and I am Edward Rose. Who leads your party?"

A large man, with a big buffalo rifle in the crook of his arm, answered. "I am John Daugherty," said the stranger. "We have been trappin the Yellowstone, but those damn Blackfeet have about eaten us alive. Those bastards killed two of my best men and stole our horses and traps. We would be pleased to offer your men some food if you'll sit a spell." Ed and his young men dismounted and joined the trappers for supper. After exchanging information, Ed decided to travel with Daugherty for a few days.

While trapping near the junction of *Otter* Creek, they met a band of Hidatsa returning from a raid. Ed learned from them that they had also fought with the same Blackfoot party that Daugherty encountered. He obtained fresh meat for them but asked their war chief, Rainbird, to move on two miles before setting up their camp.

Ed then turned to Daugherty. "John," he said, "we will have to pen our horses and set out some night watches. Those Hidatsa will come back tonight and try to take our mounts." Daugherty ordered all their animals to be hobbled and penned. He assigned four watches to guard the camp through the night. However, this night was dark and cold and the Hidatsa warriors were able to sneak into their herd and steal seven of their best horses.

Ed told Daugherty, "Well John, we might as well calm down and try to get some rest. We can't do anything tonight, but we will go after them hard at first light."

As the sun rose over the low hills, Ed led seven men to pick up the trail of the fleeing Hidatsa. They located one straggler on a worn-out horse and when he saw his pursuers he jumped off the dying mustang and climbed a bluff. Ed stopped and loaded a double ball into his Hawken rifle. He sighted in and knocked the thief down at almost two hundred yards, but unfortunately the man's body lodged behind a rock. Not to be deterred,

Ed dismounted and climbed the bluff where he dislodged the thief and rolled him down the steep incline. By the time Ed could get down the hill to the thief, Ed's young followers had already scalped the man.

They remounted and continued their chase until they spotted two more of the fleeing horse thieves, a middle-aged man and a young boy. They suddenly stopped and signed that they wished to surrender. The young man gave up his weapons to Daugherty but the older man decided to fight. Ed became enraged and flew into the man with his fists flailing. The man turned out to be stronger than Ed, and they rolled around on the ground clawing tooth and toenail at each other. The other five white men rode up while the fight was still in progress.

Daugherty handed his young captive over to his men and went to the aid of Ed, but just as he reached the two combatants, one of his men shot the captive boy. This enraged the older thief so much that he became crazed and began to growl like a grizzly. Then he foamed at the mouth like a wild boar. He broke away from Ed and Daugherty and ran forty yards out onto the prairie before every loaded gun in the party unloaded on him. The mortally wounded Hidatsa continued to writhe and roll on the ground for several minutes. Finally a young trapper approached him to take his scalp, but as the trapper began to cut away the old man's hair, the old man gave a great growl and rose to his knees. His reddened eyes glared widely at the young man scalping him. Panicked, the lad leapt back and ran from him.

The rest of the party howled with laughter at the

fright of the young man but Ed stopped laughing long enough to retrieve the lad's knife and gun. The older warrior finally succumbed to his many wounds. Seeing their comrades die caused the remaining Hidatsa to release their stolen horses and flee back toward Metaharta.

Daugherty and his men packed their furs and dried buffalo jerky, then headed for Fort Lisa on the Missouri. Ed decided to go along with them because he had no trade goods left and there was no immediate reason to remain among the Crow.

After weeks of travel the party started to run out of supplies again and several of their horses came up lame. Daugherty turned to Ed. "Rose, could you find the way to Fort Lisa and get us some sow belly, flour and about five fresh mounts? Also, I sure could use some fresh coffee, if you can find any there."

Ed replied, "I can get you some camp meat but I can't steal any horses unless I can find a Cheyenne or Teton Sioux camp and I sure can't provide any coffee, but I'll be back as soon as I can."

When he reached Fort Lisa, Ed was surprised to find the fort surrounded by lodges of Cheyenne. They had laid siege to the fort because it was trading with their enemies, the Crow, Hidatsa, Mandan and Arikara. Brazenly Ed rode through the entire enemy camp before entering the gates of Fort Lisa. After he entered, he approached Andrew Drips, who appeared as nervous as a drowning man in a Missouri whirlpool.

"What in hell is goin on, Drips?" asked Ed. "How long have you been treed by these bastards?"

"Rose," he sputtered, "these hornets have had me locked up tighter than a St. Louis jail for almost two weeks now. Can you talk to them and offer them something to calm them down so we can trade?"

Ed turned to Drips, "Andrew, John Daugherty is out there with his brigade of trappers, and they are about played out. They need food and horses real bad. We need to get this mess settled quickly so I can take help to his boys."

"About the Cheyenne." Ed continued, "you call in their leaders for a powwow and I'll work out a deal with them." Drips sent out an interpreter to council with the Cheyenne. Ed made himself at home and settled down with a cup of hot coffee. It had been months since he had tasted anything as good as fresh roasted coffee. Unfortunately, John Daugherty would have to wait for his supplies and horses.

After a while ten Cheyenne chiefs, led by Yellow Hand, reluctantly came into the fort. They were sullen and defiant as they faced the black man with scars all over his face. Some recognized Ed as the warrior, Five Scalps, and others just seemed intimidated by his fierce scowl. After the gates closed, Ed approached the chiefs.

In their native tongue, Ed said, "My chiefs, you are my captives. I want you to bring in my friend, John Daugherty, and his trapping brigade, or I will decapitate you one at a time." The chiefs attempted to charge him but he was too quick. He slammed his rifle over the heads of the two Cheyenne nearest to him before they could reach him.

While the chiefs were still in shock, Andrew Drips called out, "My chiefs, let us negotiate. Please, Five Scalps, do not kill them because I wish to trade with them."

Chief Yellow Hand regained his composure. "Mr. Drips," he said, "if you will offer my people presents and open honest trade, we will accept Chief Five Scalps' conditions." Relieved, Drips immediately provided Northwest blankets and cloth to the chiefs.

Yellow Hand then offered, "Release me and I will bring in John Daugherty and his men to prove our trust. We will then trade with you." Drips released six horses loaded with supplies to the chief and allowed him to leave the fort. There was an uneasy truce among the remaining Cheyenne chiefs until Chief Yellow Hand and Daugherty returned several days later.

Daugherty said to Ed and Drips, "Boys, when I saw those Cheyenne warriors come into our camp I thought we were goners for sure. However, we needed those supplies and horses so badly, we had no choice except to trust them, and they were helpful to us."

After peace had been settled between Fort Lisa and the Cheyenne, Drips said, "We must get our furs back to St. Louis. Rose, why don't you take them? You said you don't have any pressing business in the mountains."

Ed answered, "Well I don't have any trade goods and I sure could use some new credit in St. Louis, so I reckon I'll just ride with your men, but only as far as the Rees. I don't think I am ready for St. Louis yet."

CHAPTER 13

Manuel Lisa led his engages up the Missouri as quickly as they could pole and pull their keelboats. He intended to catch up with Wilson Price Hunt's Astorians to protect his large trade enterprise in the foothills of the Rockies. He had old Toussaint Charbonneau along as his interpreter.

Lisa finally located the Astorians at the villages of the Arikara. He invited Pierre Dorion, Hunt's guide, to his campfire.

"*Senor* Dorion," he began, "come drink with me, my *amigo*." Dorion was guarded but polite. Lisa had never been particularly fond of him.

Trying to remain civil, Dorion replied, "*Oui! Monsieur.* I will drink with you for old times."

Lisa asked, "Are you satisfied with your engagement with *Senor* Hunt?"

Dorion began, "*Oui, Monsieur.* Although *Monsieur* Hunt does not take my advice, he pays well and assures me of a fine position in Astoria, once we reach the Columbia River. He has angered the Ree for being too cheap with his gifts and not selling them firearms. However, I have recommended he retain *Monsieur* Edward Rose to smooth relations here and obtain the necessary horses to take us to the Rockies."

Lisa sipped his port wine and puffed on his pipe. He knew first hand how volatile Rose could be, and perhaps Rose would kill Hunt with his bare hands, like he tried to do to him in 1808 at Fort Raymond.

Lisa coyly offered, "*Si, Senor* Dorion. Rose is the right man at the right time to guide your party. He is still a chief among the Ree as well as among the Crow. I will contact Major Henry to release him from any other employment at once."

Dorion said, "That will not be necessary, *Monsieur.* Edward Rose resides in the village of Chief Little Soldier. I will contact him shortly now that you have released him."

Lisa offered, "Well, then tell *Senor* Hunt that my brigade stands ready to defend him against the hostility of the Ree if the need should arise." When Dorion informed Hunt of his conversation with Lisa, Hunt was pleased but skeptical. Hunt was just naturally paranoid and did not trust anyone.

Hunt asked Dorion, "How do I know this Rose will not spy on us for Lisa and sell us out to the first Indian tribe we encounter?"

"Do not worry, *Monsieur* Hunt," Dorion responded. "Rose once tried to kill *Monsieur* Lisa for insulting his honesty and integrity. *Monsieur* Rose is an Arikara war chief as well as a Crow war chief. He is fluent in their languages and has much influence with them. He also knows the mountains and its inhabitants better than any American around. He will get us the horses we need and he will get us to the Columbia on time." Hunt relied upon Dorion and went around his camp checking on their security and food supplies while Dorion prayed that Five Scalps would be on his best behavior. He knew how dangerous his friend could be when riled by someone like Hunt.

Dorion was angry with Lisa for trying to bribe him away from Hunt. As he began drinking some of the rum he had hidden away, he saw Lisa approaching the Astorian camp.

Lisa, said, "*Senor* Dorion, I remind you that if you do not accept my employ, I must ask you to pay your old debt to me for alcohol. I cannot continue to carry expenses for anyone who is opposed to me."

That did it. Dorion flew into a frenzy, aided by the warmth of the rum. He knocked Lisa to the ground, where upon Lisa leaped to his feet screaming, "Where is my knife? Where is my gun? I will kill you for being a deadbeat son-of-a-bitch."

While Lisa ran to get his weapons, Dorion armed himself with two pistols. A crowd began to gather, including Ramsay Crooks and Robert McClellan, who encouraged Dorion to continue the feud with Lisa.

When Hunt arrived upon the scene it was all he could do to keep both camps from attacking each other. In the end, it was two guest travelers who finally restored the peace. They were hunter-writer Henry Brackenridge and naturalist John Bradbury.

CHAPTER 14

There was little communication between the two camps as they held to an uneasy truce. Lisa sent one of his engages to the Arikara villages. "Locate *Senor* Rose," he ordered, "and tell him I need him urgently."

As Ed rode down the river to the camps of the two white parties, he called to the pickets on guard. "Hello there! I'm Edward Rose. Take me to Mr. Lisa at once."

At Lisa's tent he found a frightened *bourgeois*, his old employer. "Well, I'm here, *Senor* Lisa," Ed said. "Will you employ me again?"

"No," Lisa responded. "I wish you to guide Price Hunt and his Astorians to the Pacific Ocean. I do not wish them to interfere with the Missouri trade because I control the river now."

Ed's eyes lit up. "Where is this eastern dude you want me to guide?"

Lisa sputtered, "I almost killed the *pendejo*. However, he needs you to obtain horses for him and to calm the Rees, because they are threatening both of our companies. *Senor* Rose, we need your influence. You will find Hunt's camp at the very large tent near the *rio*."

As Ed approached the tent, he saw a medium-sized man with cold, blue eyes and thin, down-turned lips. His eyes darted around nervously, as though having difficulty focusing on the people he was addressing. He seemed intense.

"I am Ed Rose," said Ed, introducing himself. "I have come from the Arikara to help you fellows out. What can I do for you, Captain?"

Hunt exhaled and said, "Mr. Rose I have heard many things about you and most of them are not good. If I had my way, I would stay as far away from you as I could get."

Hunt paused and then continued. "My partners and I have formed the Pacific Fur Company. Our enterprise has a keelboat and a Schenectady barge loaded with supplies. We have two hundred gallons of whiskey, ample gunpowder, two hundred pounds of lead, six barrels of flour, fifty bushels of corn, and a thousand pounds of biscuits. We also have axes, hoes, lanterns, a canoe adz, sweet oil, paregoric, opium, mercury ointment, muskets, rifles and one howitzer. Plus, we have some presents and trade goods."

"My major partner is Mr. Jacob Astor," Hunt explained, "but we also have Alexander McKay, Duncan McDougal, Donald Mackenzie, Robert Stuart and some minor investors. Others in my employ are Picotte, LaLiberte, Delorme, Lapensee, Roussel, Perrault, Robilliard, Franchere, McGillis, de Montigny, Pillet, Farnham,

Stuart, Ross and of course your friend, Pierre Dorion. He speaks well of you. If you can get me a hundred fifty horses, I will employ you to take my party to the Columbia River on the Pacific Coast. Can you deliver?"

Ed held his temper. He wanted to kick the dung out of the pompous ass. Instead he replied, "I'll do the best I can, Captain. I'll go see some of my contacts right away." Ed could not go to Little Soldier because the chief controlled few horses; therefore he had to go to Grey Eyes. So he rode toward the Arikara lodges at Rhtarahe, where he approached his half-breed friend, Joseph Garreau. Garreau had lived among the Arikara for over twenty years and had great influence among them.

Ed greeted Garreau. "Well, how the hell are you, Joe? How is your influence with Grey Eyes? Is he at war with everybody or just most whites?"

Garreau chuckled. "Come on in, *Monsieur* Rose," he said. "I am a neutral man who tries to keep his hair, no? He is badly influenced by his civil chief, *Le Gauche* and his war chief, Big Man. Surely you remember them, no? How can I help the famous Chief Five Scalps?"

"Well, I need a job and I have this jackass white man who wants to pay me good money to get him one hundred and fifty horses. Can you help me for a fee?"

"I do not know, *Monsieur.* This Hunt has been so cheap that he has insulted Chief Grey Eyes. I will speak to him, but Grey Eyes is very angry. The Ree have joined with the Mandan and Hidatsa in an attempt to close the river to white men's traffic. They want weapons and no one will trade with them, and yet their enemies - the

Sioux, Teton and Dakota - get their guns from my North-west Company. However, I cannot get my own outfit to provide guns to the Ree, Hidatsa or Mandan. It is mad-dening, *Monsieur.*"

"Well, do what you can for old time's sake," asked Ed. "I'll meet you here tomorrow mornin."

"*Oui, Monsieur.* I will do my best for an old friend." Ed returned to camp to take care of his own horses and gear before some French boatman helped himself to his property. It seemed the Canadians were bigger thieves than the Crow.

At dawn, Ed rode back to Rhtarahe where he spotted Garreau and rode directly to him. He tied his horse to a large picket before asking, "Well, where do we stand?"

Garreau slowly offered, "I think you should deal directly with Grey Eyes. He seems to have some trust of you, but he has hatred for the man called Hunt." With that Ed followed the Frenchman into the encampment. They entered a large earth lodge where the chiefs were seated around a small council-fire. Ed addressed Grey Eyes, Le Gauche and Big Man.

"My chiefs," he offered, "I need your kind assis-tance. Remember that I have been a war chief among you and brought you many honors and many horses. Chief Grey Eyes, is it not true that when we last parted I freely gave you many fine horses to add to your wealth?"

"It is so, my friend," he answered. "You have always spoken true words and done good deeds for our people. However, my friend, we are losing our trade with the

Shoshoni, Crow, Flathead, Nez Perce and other tribes to the white men. We care not for the furs they take from our mountain streams and we even forgive them for destroying our game and leaving their diseases among our women. But we cannot abide the white men taking trade from us and arming our enemies, without providing us with guns, lead and powder to defend ourselves. Can you help us?"

Ed puffed the council pipe to the four directions. "My chiefs, I will get you lead and powder. I will get you cloth, vermilion, awls and knives."

Chief Grey Eyes rose and said, "Chief Five Scalps, we will provide as many horses as we can spare. It is true we can steal more, but our enemies are getting stronger and they have guns while we do not. *Monsieur* Garreau will bring you your horses with the morning sun. Be careful my friend."

With that, the chief excused Ed, who left the lodge with Garreau and returned to where he had tied his horse. At least his animal was still where he had left it. At dawn, Ed observed Joe Garreau approach with a small herd of average ponies. Ed counted thirty animals and feared that Hunt would surely fire him after only his second day of employment.

"Garreau, is that the best Grey Eyes can do?"

The Frenchman meekly replied, "*Monsieur*, it is the best anyone could do. The other chiefs counseled Grey Eyes to declare war instead of sending you these lowly animals. Only your friendship with the chiefs has brought you this concession. Now, what can I give the chiefs in return?"

"Well," Ed hesitated, "I couldn't do much either. I did get three kegs of powder, one keg of flints, one keg of lead, some knives, some awls and some vermilion. However, after lookin at your horses, I think the chiefs got the best of the deal, don't you?"

He and Garreau both laughed at the whole affair. If the atmosphere between the Arikara and the traders did not change, conflict would have to come to the river.

By July 1811, Hunt was far behind schedule. Although he was disgusted with the trade Ed had made with the village, he decided to retain Rose with the hopes that he could assist them in gaining more horses from other tribes when they reached the plains.

Ed had the tails of each new horse bobbed and their manes trimmed in order to identify them as belonging to Hunt's brigade. Ed felt sure the natives wouldn't want bob-tailed nags like these, because they placed great importance upon long hair on their person as well as their horses.

Hunt then traded his barge, keelboat and howitzer to Lisa for some additional horses that Lisa said he could get from the Mandan. But, even Lisa could only obtain fifty additional mounts. Hunt now had a total of eighty-two horses when he actually needed well over a hundred.

CHAPTER 15

It was July 18th when Ed led the Astorians up the Grand River, along a prairie where grass was knee-high and lush. When they occasionally lost the trail, they found the grass almost impenetrable. By the time they reached Firesteel Creek, many in the party were ill. Ramsay Crooks was so sick that Hunt had to make camp for a week to give him enough time to recuperate. They desperately needed more mounts for those who became sick. Too many of the ill had to walk and they were not getting well due to the strain.

Hunt finally sent Benjamin Jones, John Day and Ed Rose to trade with the northern Cheyenne. On July 26th they found a large Cheyenne village. Being able to speak some of their language and using sign language, Ed was able to obtain thirty-six additional horses by trading cloth, beads, knives and hide scrapers to the Cheyenne.

When the trading party caught up with the Astorians, Hunt thanked Ed, but he threw in, "Mr. Rose, you obtained better animals here than you did from the Arikara. However, don't be so liberal with my trade goods." Ed did a slow burn, but he held his temper in check. He had obtained very fine horses from one of his oldest enemies and still his employer complained. He felt like allowing the Cheyenne to steal the animals back that very night, but instead, he doubled the nightly horse guard.

The expedition moved at the rate of twenty to twenty-five miles each day. The terrain became dryer, more rocky and offered shorter grass, but they also encountered their first large buffalo herds. They struggled over Slim Buttes and headed for the Little Missouri River, where they could see the Powder River Range in the hazy distance.

They left Box Elder Creek and pushed over the rugged Powder ridges and over the northern tip of the Missouri Buttes, where they saw bighorn sheep for the first time. Ed guided the brigade toward the northeastern portion of Thunder Basin, where it was lush with grass, watered by numerous streams. Here they found that game was plentiful. In this area they found gooseberries, currants and chokecherries. Not only did they find buffalo and elk, but they found that white-haired grizzlies were also numerous and dangerous.

Thunder Basin was bounded on the east by the Bear Lodge Mountains and on the west by the Bighorn Mountains. By August 20th the party reached Prairie Creek. That night their water buckets contained a quarter inch of ice, suggesting an early winter. But the days were still plenty warm.

After Ed located the Crow trading trail, he led the party through familiar territory. It turned so unseasonably hot that Mackenzie's dog died of heat exhaustion, and several of his men suffered from lack of water and shade. By August 28th the group approached the Bighorn Mountains where they fire-dried meat before ascending Crazy Woman Creek.

On August 30th two Crow hunters approached and warmly greeted Ed. The next day several more of his old friends arrived, making Hunt quite nervous. Hunt feared that Ed was plotting to betray him to the natives and take all their horses and goods. His fearful paranoia caused him to think some of his men were too friendly with Rose and that they might be induced to join Rose in that betrayal. Hunt was especially suspicious of Alexander Carson, Louis St. Michael, Pierre Detaye and Pierre Delounay.

Hunt told McClellan, "I believe Rose is a bad person who is full of adventure and treachery, and when we reach the main Crow village, I am going to fire him."

McClellan responded, "Fire him hell! Let's just shoot the black bastard. I'll have John Reed do it."

Hunt responded quickly. "No, I don't want to make him a martyr. That would rile the Crow against us."

In September they located the main Crow village and after four days of celebrating and trading, Hunt pulled Ed aside. "Mr. Rose," he began, "I will not need your services anymore. Pierre Dorion can guide our brigade on to the Columbia River. I will leave you here, among the Crow, but I will pay you a half year's wage, which will consist of one horse, three beaver traps and some trade goods."

Ed's anger burned, but he controlled his temper. "Well," he said, "we don't see eye-to-eye anyway, so I'll take your offer with no hard feelins. However, I urge you to hire a Crow guide to take you across the southern pass. It's a lot easier than passing over the Rockies. Those passes can be deadly when the snows come."

Hunt did not trust Rose or his recommendations and would take his chances with Dorion. Ed was disappointed that he would not see the Pacific Ocean, but he also realized that sooner or later he probably would have killed Hunt. Ed found the man arrogant, obsessive and controlling. Hunt even wanted to control those things of which he had no knowledge. Ed muttered to himself, "That man will die in the Snake River country before he ever reaches the Columbia River." He knew that if the Astorians did not move quickly, they could not cross the Rockies before the mountains closed for the winter. Ed also knew that game was scarce in the high country.

After Hunt and his party left, Ed settled back into life in Absaroka. He led a band of his Crow braves on a horse raid over the Bighorn Mountains. When they approached Ten Sleep Pass, they found the tracks of the Astorians, where they had obviously missed going into the Wind River Mountains. When Hunt saw Rose's party, he feared for his life, and almost ordered his men to fire on him. However, he controlled himself and waited for

Rose to make the first move.

"Hey there Captain," Ed called out, "you boys are a might off track, aren't you? I think you might want to travel down that ridge over there and you can pick up the main tradin trail."

Hunt turned to Dorion. "Is Mr. Rose correct, Pierre?" Dorion looked confused and nervous.

"*Monsieur* Hunt," said Dorion, "I defer to Five Scalps. No one knows these *monts* better than he, no?" Ed directed them down along Nowood Creek where they were able to obtain game, good grass for their horses, and many berries to supplement their diet of red meat.

Ed told Dorion, "When you reach the Wind River, ascend it to Little Warm Springs. There you can follow the trail up over Union Pass, where you can locate the headwaters of the Green River. If you miss it to the north, you will wind up on the Gros Ventre and it will still take you to the Snake River, but it is out of the way by quite a bit. Take care of Marie and your kids and to hell with Hunt."

Dorion bowed his embarrassed face to Ed and said, "Thank you, *Monsieur*. I hope I can keep *Monsieur* Hunt on the trail, but he continues to countermand my advice and to misjudge the terrain."

As the group rode on down the main trail, Ed guided his raiding party back over Ten Sleep and down Crazy Woman Creek. They were looking for Cheyenne or Teton camps that they could raid for some new horses. Again Ed murmured, "Those poor bastards will never reach the Pacific Ocean."

CHAPTER 16

While the mountains grew colder and the snow deeper, the River Crow bellies grew smaller and ached from hunger. They were in dire need of fresh meat and protein. On a hunting trip, Ed took some of his Big Dog warriors and crossed the Yellowstone, above the Horses River. Riding past Rattlesnake Butte, they found no sign of bison, the lifeline for the natives living on the plains. Ed decided they must search out the valleys on the Musselshell if they were to find game. It took two days of continuous riding before they reached the round valley north of the Musselshell.

With terribly bad timing, some young Atsina boys rode across the valley chasing a good size buffalo herd when they saw Ed and his experienced Crow hunters. The young Atsinas scattered in all directions, as did the herd of buffalo they were chasing.

Ed laughed. He yelled to his party, "Scare the brave young hunters but do not harm them. We only want the buffalo to take home, but if you can, grab a few of their horses." Ed and his men gave chase, yelling and firing their guns when they had a good shot at cow. Many of Ed's men still used bows when hunting, which was dangerous, because they needed well-trained buffalo chasing horses and they had to ride very close in order to drive the arrows into the heart of the lumbering beasts.

When Ed stopped to get his wind and rest his horse, Spotted Pony rode up to him. Steam billowed from the nostrils of his tired horse. The man gasped, "Come, Five Scalps. Cracked-Ice needs you now! He has found something interesting and he needs your advice." Ed was puzzled. What could an experienced warrior like Cracked-Ice need from him? Had he captured one of the young hunters or had one of his men become injured? He followed Spotted Pony, who led him over a rise.

Soon Ed saw Yellow Belly and Cracked-Ice holding the reins of three strange horses, one of them a fine stallion. As he drew closer, he noticed that they were also holding one of the young hunters, who struggled mightily, trying to get away.

Cracked-Ice said, "Five Scalps, I did not know what I should do because my captive is a young girl! Not only is she a girl, but she speaks our language. She claims she is a Crow who was captured by the Atsina." As Ed dismounted, he noticed the girl looking at him fearfully. She kept staring at him, watching his every move. She slowly quit struggling and seemed as if she were going to speak, but before she could, Ed spoke to her.

In Crow, Ed asked, "What are you called? I am called

Five Scalps of the River Sparrowhawks."

The young girl tried to stand tall as she replied in Crow. "I am called Shining Sun of the White Clay people who live on the Milk River. We have been hunting buffalo for our starving people. I am Crow, but I was captured by the Atsina when I was very young, and my parents and relatives were all killed by the raiding 'Big Bellies'." Ed observed her closely and then turned her around. It was true that she was well formed and had fine features, and even looked more like the Crow tribe than the Atsina tribe.

Ed asked her, "Why were you with the young hunting party? Do the Atsina use women to hunt while their men do the cooking and lodge work?" He hoped he could shame her into telling the truth and discover what she was really up to. Instead, she seemed even more confident and stood proud as she spoke.

"I was adopted by Chief Black Elk because I was a Sparrowhawk," she said. "He gave me bows and these three fine stallions and allowed me to be trained as a hunter. He hoped my Sparrowhawk blood would provide leadership and example for his own warriors." Ed smiled at her audacity, but decided to humor the young girl. He had defeated the Atsina many times and felt that they fought more like women than men, so perhaps Chief Black Elk was trying to shame them into becoming better fighters. He had no way of knowing that this girl had learned Crow from a young River Crow woman, who actually had been captured by her father, One Ear. Being creative and a survivalist, she played the role of

103

her adopted mother, Red Plum, as well as she could.

Because of her confidence, her appearance and her fluency in the Crow language, Ed decided to accept her story. He directed his men to butcher and pack their fresh kills and then he led the entire party back to Absaroka, taking the girl and her horses with him.

Following Crow custom, the young captive girl rode behind Cracked-Ice, the brave who had captured her. Yellow Belly was also entitled to become her adopted brother and protector, but he was not interested in doing so because he did not believe her story. He was angry, intractable and distrustful of most things, and he did not believe one thing this ridiculous young captive told them. He respected Five Scalps as a warrior, but after all, he was still a 'white man'.

Crow culture provided that a captive had to be adopted by the captor, and that the capturing braves must become the captive's protectors and teachers. None of the captors could ever marry the captive.

While they rode toward Absaroka, Shining Sun questioned Cracked-Ice about everything she could think of in order to gain more knowledge about their tribe. Red Plum had told her as much as she could, but it was obvious to Shining Sun that she needed much more information if she were to carry on her charade.

She learned that her new brother was from a village called *Mine'sepere*, and his clan was Dung-on-the-River-Banks. Cracked-Ice said it was his mother's clan, but he had to marry outside of her clan and join his new wife's clan. He told her the Crow were matrilineal in culture.

Shining Sun knew that the Atsina had a patrilineal culture. Among the Crow, the mother owned all property and was the center of family life.

Shining Sun had a reason for being so inquisitive about the tribe. The girl had secretly vowed that she would not become a wife or mother. Instead of being a lodge woman, she wanted to become a warrior and hunter, and she was willing to do this no matter what the cost. She questioned Cracked-Ice about the strong, black man with the many facial battle scars and she learned why he was named Five Scalps.

After ascending the Bighorn River for two suns Shining Sun saw smoke plumes curling lazily into the bright sky. Under the clouds of smoke lay three hundred oddly shaped lodges that looked like the lodgepoles had been extended on top of the lodges to almost form another uncovered lodge.

As they rode into the village, a crowd formed around them. Children began yelling and running about while all the dogs barked. Ed stopped near the lodge of Arapooash, dismounted and entered.

"Chief Rotten Belly," he spoke, "we have captured a strange girl from our enemy, the Atsina. She claims to have been taken captive from us in a raid about five snow-seasons ago. She also claims to be a hunter. I think you should see her."

Rotten Belly stared into his sacred fire. Five Scalps was indeed intelligent, fearless and not easily fooled; if Five Scalps thought this captive was a Sparrowhawk, then the chief knew he must interview her. Finally, the chief said, "Bring this girl captive to me."

Cracked-Ice and Yellow Belly escorted their captive into the chief's lodge while Rotten Belly continued to sit on his robes and smoke his pipe. He stared intently into the red flames of his lodge-fire, then looked up at the small girl. He was surprised to see that she was attractive, with large round and inquisitive eyes.

The chief asked, "Who are your people?"

Struggling to retain her composure, Shining Sun replied, "Oh, great chief, my parents were slain by the Atsina when they raided our village on the Horses River five seasons ago. My mother hid me in a plum thicket before the cowardly Atsina killed her, and then their famous warrior, One Ear, captured me and gave me to Chief Black Elk, who adopted me." Rotten Belly had heard of One Ear and he had fought against Chief Black Elk. The girl continued, "The Atsina stole many Sparrowhawk horses and drove them for days to their villages on the Milk River. I do not have any relatives who lived."

The wise chief stared into her eyes before finally nodding. He remembered such a raid. At least twenty of his people had been killed and the Sparrowhawks had lost over seventy horses. He thought, "Surely this young maiden must be one of our people and I must welcome her back to our village with a festival and a dance."

He then rose from his robes and declared, "As our custom dictates, Five Scalps will become our new captive's teacher. My brother, Yellow Belly and his friend, Cracked-Ice shall become her adopted brothers and protectors."

The angry Yellow Belly grunted. "I decline this custom. I am too busy leading and training the Big Dogs, and I do not believe this captive. I think she is the spoiled child of some Atsina chief and has concocted this entire tale. She learned our language by torturing one of our own people. I, Yellow Belly, have spoken."

After Yellow Belly's outburst, Shining Sun became frightened. Had her story been discredited? Was she in danger for her life? She waited without even allowing herself to breathe. Rotten Belly sighed. His younger brother was negative and disagreeable about most things, and had been so since his birth. Yellow Belly was jealous of his older brother because he could never seem to follow in Rotten Belly's giant footsteps.

Rotten Belly said, "My brother, it is your privilege to decline your responsibilities if you wish. So be it." The chief then turned to the pale Shining Sun and asked, "Do you wish anything my child?"

"Yes, my father," she stammered, "I wish to retain ownership of my three fine horses and my gun, because they were given to my by Chief Black Elk." She took a deep breath, regained her composure, and continued. "I was a member of the Hammer Owner Society among the Atsina, and I would like to join that society among the Sparrowhawks."

Before Rotten Belly could recover from Shining Sun's request, she started reciting the rituals she had learned from her adoptive mother, Red Plum. Rotten Belly could not believe the brashness of this exasperating young girl. The bellicose Yellow Belly stormed out of the chief's lodge.

Rotten Belly meditated on the ever-widening turn of events. Quietly he reasoned, "It is true that the Atsina Hammer Owner rituals sounded similar to the Sparrowhawks own society; however, our people have never allowed females to be trained as hunters or warriors. This would be a precedent-setting decision."

Meanwhile, Ed Rose smiled. How would the chief handle this strange situation? Personally, he felt women were good for only one thing, but if he met one who was strong enough and brave enough to fight along side of him, he would certainly accept her.

Rotten Belly struggled with his decision. He wondered, "If the Atsina chose to accept her as a warrior, perhaps it will be a great omen. After all, the Great Spirit has returned her to us and her medicine seems strong."

At last the chief spoke. "My secret-helper tells me that our daughter has been returned to us to bring us good fortune. Five Scalps and Cracked-Ice shall tutor and train her. If she proves unsuited for battle, they can make that determination before any harm has been done to Sparrowhawk order."

Cracked-Ice was thrilled with his new position and responsibility. He liked the cocky, confident young girl and treated her like a younger sister. However Ed was not particularly happy about his new responsibility. He felt there was still a great deal of mystery about this girl. He went along with Rotten Belly's assignment in order to please the chief. Besides, he did not know how long he would remain among the River Crow.

In the end, Ed said, "This future warrior-woman must have a true Sparrowhawk name. I propose she be called *Bar-che-ampe,* our beloved Pine Leaf."

Rotten Belly, relieved to have Five Scalps agree with his ruling, said, "It is so my people. Forever more, our sister, whom the Great Spirit has returned to us, shall be known as 'Pine Leaf'."

CHAPTER 17

As the winter of 1811 grew cold and icy, the two great Crow tribes joined at the hot springs on the Bighorn River. When the tribes met, jubilant cries of, "Ka'he! Ka'he!" rang out. As Chief Long Hair and Chief Rotten Belly organized their camps, they assigned the police and designated hunting parties to bring in fresh game for the winter food supply. After four days of celebrating and renewing old acquaintances, the villagers settled down.

In the middle of a cold December night, Ed was jolted out of his bedroll by howling dogs. Soon women and children started to shriek and cry. Warriors wrestled with their horses as the animals bolted from their shackles and halter ropes. Warriors tried to catch them but they themselves could not stand upright. Although the shaking lasted less than a minute, to Ed it seemed much longer. As he stood outside his tent, Ed realized they had experienced an earthquake. He had heard them described but had not expected anything like this.

Long Hair ran from his lodge calling, "Be calm my people. It is our Spirit Mother rebelling for our abuse of her. She is adjusting the fire in her belly. Several times in my life I have experienced an occurrence like this. As a result, I have tried to live my life better in order to calm her." He paused briefly, and then continued. "Now we must pledge ourselves not to exploit her trees, water or game. I believe she will be repeating her shaking for two full moons to test our resolve, so take care of your families and your animals before Spirit Mother shakes again."

The people gathered their horses and everyone slowly calmed, but before they could become complacent, they experienced more shocks, some almost as strong as the first. As Long Hair had predicted, the shocks lasted into the late winter of 1812.

In the spring, Ed started training some of the young Hammer Owner Society members. He also trained his protégé, Pine Leaf. The young girl was so confident and eager that she fascinated him. She was the most intelligent member of the Hammer Owner group. Ed aided his friend, Cracked-Ice, by assigning Pine Leaf to guard the horse herd, which included moving them to fresh grass. If there was no grass, she was to gather cottonwood bark for them to eat and to take them water. The girl was allowed to groom and ride her own mounts, Black Hand, Spotted Nose and Thunder.

When Pine Leaf rode Thunder, she and the big black stallion could out-race any of the boys in the Hammer Owner Society. Ed wondered why a chief would let his young daughter have a highly trained buffalo-chaser as her personal mount. He either had many horses or else he spoiled her unbelievably. From what he had seen of the Atsina, even their fine warriors did not ride horses like Thunder.

Pine Leaf enjoyed the open air of Absaroka and tried to be competitive with the boys. She often became depressed and even entertained thoughts of returning to her White Clay people. However, she knew that Five Scalps and the Crow warriors could easily track her down and recapture her if she left. She missed her friend, Little Feather, and promised herself that someday she would return to her people and share her Crow experiences.

Pine Leaf loved Cracked-Ice and followed him everywhere, but she admired Five Scalps. She tried to please him and eagerly obeyed his every command. His Big Dog society consisted of the most mature and experienced warriors among the River Crow. She learned that Five Scalps was paired off with Yellow Belly, who was also a fearless war leader.

Pine Leaf watched the Big Dog Society members use a stick about four large hands long covered with buckskin. A pendant of deer hooves was attached to a stick. Rattles rolled with white ermine skin and topped with a down feather were attached to each end. Many members wore an owl feather headdress and all members had eagle-bone whistles hung on a thong draped around their necks. They blew their whistles continuously during their dances.

During the Big Dog ceremonies, Five Scalps and Yellow Belly led the processions, followed by two rear men and four sash-owners. Single sash owners wore one sash and two sash wearers wore their sashes crossed in front. Cracked-Ice and Tall Eagle wore belts of skin; they were called belt-wearers. They daubed their bodies with mud and tied their hair on the sides of their heads to resemble bear's ears. They were required to walk up to an enemy and rescue a fellow clansman from harm. Due to the danger of their role, they were allowed to eat first at all feasts and to dance first at all society dances. Tall Eagle and Cracked-Ice were highly regarded as future war leaders.

Ed became more tolerant of Pine Leaf the more he worked with her. He even discussed battle strategy with the young girl. He discussed his belief in many of the Crow customs, although he deplored self-mutilation during mourning. He told her, "You can never become a great warrior if you cut off your fingers. Never harm yourself. Instead, just get even. If enemies should harm or kill my friends, I will pursue them to their death, but I will not cut myself."

Ed was amazed at her accuracy with bow and arrow and he liked her three-fingered pull so much that he began using it himself. He found the new method improved his accuracy and allowed him to pull a much more powerful bow. He restored her rifle to her and began to instruct her on the use of the weapon by teaching her how to aim, shoot and clean the gun.

To Pine Leaf, Five Scalps was always serious. She

noticed he did not join in with the other warriors in telling tall tales, ribald jokes or making fun of each other. She noticed that no one poked fun at Five Scalps.

By late spring, Pine Leaf was officially inducted into the Hammer Owner Society. She already out-ran, out-rode and out-smarted most of the boys in the society and she was growing taller. Ed decided that the girl was not a beauty, but she had fine features and her spirit seemed to soar. No one in Absaroka could help but notice her aura and her presence. She held much of the same traits that Ed himself exhibited when he came to Absaroka to live with the Crow. He believed that this girl would bear watching as she matured.

After the ice broke up on the rivers, a group of traders traveled up the Yellowstone to the Little Bighorn. The River Crow welcomed the newcomers and eagerly began to trade and barter for their goods. Ed greeted Frances Antoine Larocque, a man he had known for some time.

In his best French, Ed said, "Halloo, *Monsieur* Larocque! What brings the great French trader into Crow country?"

Antoine responded, "*Monsieur* Rose, or should I refer to you as Chief Five Scalps? I have brought Charles MacKenzie and John Evans of the North West Company with me to show them the best trapping and hunting country in the Rockies."

Ed smiled. "Here comes Chief Rotten Belly. Let me do the interpreting so I can appear to be important. Be sure to give the chief some nice gifts so he can look good to his people."

It was easy for Ed to leverage Larocque because Ed led him to believe that the Hudson Bay Company was also very generous with the Crow and coveted their trade. The Hudson Bay Company had almost bankrupted the North West Company in the Oregon Territory as well as in Canada. Therefore, it was important for Larocque to keep his trade on the Red River of the North and on the upper Missouri River. The Frenchmen held a feast and traded with the Crow for two days. The Crow traded for traps, shot, powder, knives, needles and other essentials. The Crow in return gave most of their skins, hides and furs to the Frenchmen. They even traded some of their beautiful beaded shoes, along with possible bags, paunches, quivers, and buckskin clothing. The Frenchman believed that Crow beadwork was the best of all the tribes on the plains.

When Larocque and his partners departed, Ed and Cracked-Ice resumed hunting and training the young Hammer Owners. One day Cracked-Ice told Pine Leaf, "All braves must enter the sweat-lodge for purification prior to a raid and they must drink a lot of water to thin their blood. They must pray to their secret-helpers, which can be a special rock wrapped in doeskin, or a whistle made from an eagle's bone."

He continued, "Before they raid they must have new moccasins made to wear home after the raid. They should take along a dog to carry their shoes, ropes and their war shirt. The dog might even carry a small paunch of water for them. Scouts are called 'aktsite' and they wear wolfskins so they can imitate and howl like wolves. During a raid, warriors must go without food and make a camp called 'actatse', which is usually constructed with sticks, bark and foliage. The raiding party should send out scouts while the rest of the party sleeps. When the scouts return, they will kick over piles of buffalo dung and report what they have found. Party members then eat meat, tie sacred objects to their bodies, paint their faces and sing towards the enemy camp. One of the group will then be chosen to lead the party in the raid."

Cracked-Ice continued tutoring his little sister. "After a raid, warriors ride or run at full-speed, night and day, until they get home. A celebration pudding called 'batsikyarakua' is prepared for the homecoming feast. A long dance or 'bahatsge' is held with young women sitting behind the warriors singing 'tsura' songs. Raids or 'duxias' are usually brought on by a vision, by revenge or by a raid planner called 'akduxigyutsgye'. The number of his followers determines the proven bravery of a leader. Scalps are scraped, dried and blackened with charcoal and placed on a stick, but when warriors recite deeds, they can never boast of scalps. They can tell of 'dakce', or counting of coup on the enemy, by touching him with your hands or with your coup stick. If one of you excels all others you will be referred to as *'kambasakace'.*'"

Ed and Cracked-Ice sheltered Pine Leaf in their lodge, which consisted of twenty fir lodge-poles each about twenty feet long. The poles crossed at the smoke-hole opening, creating an hourglass appearance. Their lodge was covered with sixteen buffalo hides, painted with illustrious scenes of the inhabitants' accomplishments. Five Scalp's depictions were the most prominent. However, Cracked-Ice would soon have a new scene on his lodge, the capture and return of his adopted sister, Pine Leaf.

Ed taught Pine Leaf many of the white man's ways but he left Crow culture up to Cracked-Ice. Ed beamed with pride in the early summer when Pine Leaf was inducted into the Hammer Owner society. Highly competitive, she could shoot arrows as accurately as any of the young men. When she rode Thunder, she out-raced all the other horses among the Hammer Owners.

Ed turned her training over to Cracked-Ice while he made plans to head back down the river to St. Louis. He was curious about any damage that may have occurred in St. Louis resulting from the winter earthquakes. He packed two of his horses with furs and hides and headed toward the Black Hills and down the Platte River.

As he slowly rode into the village of St. Charles, Ed spotted a blacksmith shop and rode up to a large white man who came away from his smoking forge to greet him. "What do you need, stranger? I'm George Casner, the smithy here. John Sutton is the only other farrier this side of St. Louis, but I'm better."

Ed dismounted and handed him the reins of his horses. "I'm Edward Rose of the Rocky Mountains. These ponies have never been shod and I want them shoed proper. Can you take care of them?"

Casner turned and called, "Jim! Boy, come over

here and unpack these animals. Get them some oats and hay and rub them down while I get my forge hot." Casner turned to Ed and said, "This Negro boy was apprenticed to me by his father, who is a prominent white feller. Jennings Beckwith was a captain in the War of Independence."

Ed observed the lad for a moment. Then Casner added, "You can get a good meal from across the street over there. I'll be a while with your mounts so you might as well relax and enjoy some good hot food."

"Thank you friend," Ed replied. "I'm interested in catchin up on the news and gossip anyway." He strolled over to the rustic café. He was pleased to find the place was clean with fresh straw covering the floor. The odors from the kitchen made his muscular stomach come back to life. He ordered a rare beefsteak with lots of potatoes and black coffee. He could not remember when he had eaten such fine fare, and when he finished he leaned back and drank more coffee.

Since no one else was in the café, the owner walked over to Ed to satisfy his curiosity about the strange mountain man. He thought Ed seemed more Indian than black, and he wanted to open conversation with him.

"Friend," said the owner, "I'm Nathaniel Boone. I own this establishment, and I've been in St. Charles for most of my life. I don't recollect seein you before."

Ed felt better than he had in months so he answered politely, "I'm Ed Rose, from the Bighorn Valley in the Rockies. I just finished guiding the Astorians to the Crow and workin for Manuel Lisa up on the Missouri.

I'm mostly a guide, interpreter and free trapper."

Boone quickly responded, "My uncle is Daniel Boone and he was quite a guide and hunter in his day. I reckon you have heard of him. He lives up the river a ways, but he is old now and doesn't hunt much anymore." He sat while Ed finished his meal, and then asked, "Say, did you folks feel any of those earthquakes?"

Ed perked up, "Hell yes, we felt them. The first one damn near scared me and the Crow to death. Was there any damage down here?"

Nathaniel replied, "The Mississippi ran backwards and brick buildings fell all over St. Louis. We heard that the village of New Madrid on the Mississippi was wiped out and that the earth sank for miles around and formed a large lake. The quakes changed the course of the Mississippi River and we are still getting reports about how far people felt the shocks and how much damage they suffered."

When Ed returned to the blacksmith shop, he walked over to the young black apprentice feeding his horses. "Boy," he asked, "How come a black boy like you is out here in the west? I here your daddy is an important white man in this country."

"Yes Sir," the young man offered. "I came here with my mamma, who is black, and my pappy, Jennings Beckwith. He apprenticed me to Mr. Casner until I am full-grown. I ain't cut out to be no blacksmith, though. I want to go to the Rockies and be a trapper and hunter, like you."

Ed smiled. "Boy," he told him, "you better learn

as much as you can right here and try to get some local trappin and huntin experience, and then maybe you
can stay alive when you hit the mountains. Don't be like
me boy, because I can't read or write. My pa was mostly
white and my ma was black and Cherokee. I can make a
living in the mountains, but I can't survive in a place like
St. Louis." Ed felt sort of sorry for the lad and wondered
what kind of life he would find on the frontier.

After staying in St. Louis for a while, Ed became
bored and decided to travel up river to visit the Omaha
tribe. He had stopped there and talked to them on his
last trip down the river, and he had enjoyed some of their
fine maidens. He could not attract a woman in St. Louis
or St. Charles, because in those cities a black man was
still considered a lower-class citizen. He would prefer
to just return to live with the natives, where the women
made him feel important and respected.

With his fur credit, Ed purchased as many trade
goods and bottles of whiskey as he could. He rode his
horse and led his pack animals to the forks of the Elk-
horn River. There, he located the Omaha lodges of Chief
Big Elk.

After courting the chief's daughter for a couple of
months, he offered her father a mule loaded with trade
goods for her hand in marriage. She was considered the
fairest maiden among the Omaha, and many young men
desired to court her. Unfortunately for Ed, Chief Black
Buffalo was one of the braves who had long sought her
hand.

When Chief Big Elk finally allowed Ed to take his daughter, White Antelope, as his wife, friction immediately worsened between Ed and Black Buffalo. Ed was quite important in the village until he ran out of cloth and beads. Once again he had very few furs to show for the trade goods he brought. With the Omaha, he thought he would become their head trader and make himself rich by giving a large number of his presents away, just like he did among the Crow and Arikara. But his plan failed. He found himself nearly destitute. As he grew more desperate and sad, he started using the only commodity he had left, his whiskey.

Ed was not normally a drinker. The alcohol made him belligerent and bellicose, and he became a trouble-maker for the trappers, traders and natives alike. In a quarrel with Black Buffalo, Ed lost his temper and hit the chief over the head with his pistol barrel. Although the chief was only stunned, the cut from the blow caused blood to stream down his face and on to his beautiful dress robes. When Chief Big Elk came to his friend's aid, Ed hit Chief Big Elk too.

By now, Ed was out of control. White Antelope ran to her father and then screamed at Ed. "Do not hurt my father anymore! Why have you injured my friend, Black Buffalo? You are no longer my husband, because I break sticks with you. I will take my lodge and you will not be allowed to enter anymore."

The camp police subdued Ed. They tied him up and then stuck him in an isolation lodge. Only Chief Big Elk kept the braves from killing his son-in-law. The chief sent some of his men down the Missouri River to locate a white party so Ed could be removed from the Omaha country.

The braves returned with Manuel Lisa's brigade commander, Joshua Pilcher. When Pilcher arrived, he commented, "I never liked that nigger. I knew he was no damn good because he was too big for his britches. Men, put him in irons. I'm going to enjoy arrestin this blackamoor and turnin him over to Commissioner Clark, who has always defended this thief." By the time Pilcher took Ed into St. Louis, William Clark had heard reports of Ed's behavior. Ed had almost single-handedly caused a war between the whites and natives on the river.

However, Manuel Lisa pleaded with Clark. "Commissioner, I will speak for *Senor* Rose and guarantee his behavior. Major Andrew Henry and I have employed him many times and we have found him invaluable. Can you not be merciful toward him?"

Clark replied, "Well, Mr. Lisa, I will release him from the stockade, but he can't reenter the Missouri River trade until he stops consuming alcohol. He has become just like the Indians in that he cannot control his liquor."

After he sobered, Ed grew sullen and bitter. He realized he had caused a great deal of trouble among the Omaha. But he felt that because he had achieved a great deal in the mountains, he should have been shown more respect regarding the Omaha incident. When Pilcher brought Ed into St. Louis in irons, Ed was devastated. Over the years he had developed tremendous confidence in his ability to achieve goals and lead people. He had never feared anything, and he had always felt he was physically and mentally up to any challenge. Now his reputation was smashed, and to make matters worse, it was his enemy, Joshua Pilcher, who had placed him under arrest.

To some degree Ed could accept that his predicament was his own fault, but not all of it. He blamed Pilcher for the way the matter was handled. He would never forgive Pilcher.

As soon as he could, Ed borrowed horses and goods from Lisa and, in disgrace, rode off toward the Osage tribe. Ed Rose swore that he would restore his reputation and would be more influential than ever.

CHAPTER 18

Ed remained in the mountains for a few seasons. After several years' absence, Ed re-entered St. Louis. This time he had enough furs for a complete new outfit and new weapons. After cleaning up, he strolled the streets to look at the busy city. Ed was glad to be in St. Louis again. He marveled at the new growth, the number of buildings and the number of people in the streets. St. Louis was really growing.

Ed picked up a newspaper and then looked for someone to read it to him. He found a young man who could read and learned that Manuel Lisa had died in 1820 and that Joshua Pilcher was the chief factor and partner of the Missouri Fur Company. Ed knew his old enemy, Pilcher, would never employ him, so he would have to seek out a new trader.

War with the British was finally over and there was a demand for good furs from the mountains. From other traders Ed learned that the French Fur Company had reorganized under Bartholomew Berthold and Pierre Chouteau. A group of Canadians who had been with the Northwest Company and Hudson's Bay Company had formed a firm called The Columbia Fur Company. The leaders were listed as William Tilton, S. S. Dudley and Kenneth Mackenzie.

Ed learned that Missouri had become a state in 1821 and Thomas Hart Benton had been elected to the United States Senate. Senator Benton supported opening the West for development and supported opening the Rocky Mountains to fur trapping enterprises. The senator wanted the United States to control the West before Great Britain could establish a more permanent claim. Since the failure of the Astorian trading post on the Columbia, the Hudson Bay Company at Fort Vancouver was in total control of the Columbia River country. This development actually pleased Ed because this meant Hunt's enterprise had failed. To his astonishment, the new towns of Franklin and Boonville had been established. The village of Lexington was now being formed way up the Missouri. It would become the furthermost outpost of civilization.

Ed was angered to learn that Missouri had become a slave-owning state. There were few free blacks in St. Louis, but Ed swore he would kill anyone who ever tried to own or sell him. He was surprised to learn that his old friend, Andrew Henry, had formed a new trading partnership with General William Ashley.

From the newspaper, the young man read this ad to Ed:

TO ENTERPRISING YOUNG MEN

The subscriber wishes to engage ONE HUNDRED MEN to ascend the river Missouri to its source, there to be employed for one, two or three years—For particulars, enquire of Major Andrew Henry, near the lead mines, in the County of Washington, (who will ascend with and command the party) or to the subscriber at St. Louis, Feb. 13th.

Wm. H. Ashley

Ed started looking for Major Henry, because he did not know General Ashley. When Ed found him, Henry said, "Well I'll be if it ain't Edward Rose. I heard you had been banned from the mountain trade by Commissioner Clark."

Ed sheepishly replied, "Yes Major, I reckon I made an ass of myself among the Omaha. However, I have been tradin among the Osage for the past few seasons and I have sworn off whiskey for good. Could you use a good man on the river?"

Henry looked Rose up and down. He could see that Ed was in good shape and well dressed for a mountain man. Ed looked like his former, fierce self. At last Henry replied, "Yes Rose, we sure could use a man of your caliber. I want you to report to General Ashley on the keelboat, *Enterprise,* down at the river wharf. He is down there procuring supplies for our trip to the Yellowstone country. I know he will be interested in your services."

Ed was excited because it had been many years since he had been on the Missouri, Yellowstone and Bighorn Rivers. He longed for his old friends and the women he had left in the mountains. He had not found the Osage women as amorous as the Crow and Arikara. With the proceeds he had made trading among the Osage, Ed purchased a new Samuel Hawkin rifle, a Hawkin pistol, and two new Green River knives. Once again he felt like a real mountain man.

He slowly paddled along the river wharf until he found a keelboat that had printing on the bow as Major Henry had described, "E-N-T-E-R-P-R-I-S-E." Ed tied his bowline to the boat's deckrail and swung his canoe around to come along side. He then called, "Hello the ship. Is there anyone aboard?"

A well-dressed man wearing a beaver hat and smoking a large cigar came out of the cabin. He was middle-aged, slim and of medium height with a thin equine nose and a strong chin. He walked on over to the rail, extended his soft pale hand and said, "Come on aboard stranger."

Ed climbed aboard the keelboat. He stuck out his hand and said, "I'm Edward Rose, the best guide and interpreter on the Missouri River. Major Henry sent me to you because he said you might want my services."

The prim and proper businessman observed the black man keenly. He observed that Rose had cold eyes, a badly scarred nose with a portion of it missing, and a gash from the corner of his mouth almost to his ear.

He obviously had been in a terrible fight at some time in his life. He figured the tall, powerfully built man looked more Indian than Negro. The General had already heard a great deal about Rose from Wilson Price Hunt. He knew that Hunt had been afraid of Ed and had paid him off when they reached the Crow in 1811. However, in St. Louis, Rose was well spoken of and was respected as a qualified interpreter among the mountain tribes.

Maintaining his decorum, Ashley answered, "I am General William Ashley of the Rocky Mountain Fur Company. I am a General in the Missouri Militia and Lieutenant Governor of the State of Missouri. I have recently formed a fur trapping expedition to the Rocky Mountains and we are indeed in need of many young men to assist us in our endeavors. However, we require a two-year commitment in the mountains."

He continued, "I have heard much of you, Rose, but some of it has not been good. Although you are highly regarded as a guide and interpreter, you have also been known as a drunkard and a troublemaker. What say you to these accusations?"

Ed was somewhat chagrined by Ashley's remarks, but he humbly answered, "I reckon some of what you heard is correct. However, I fear no one in the Rocky Mountains and I am a war chief among the Crow and the Rees. I am the only white man that they can trust, and I speak ten Indian languages as well as French and Indian sign. I have lived on the Missouri, the Bighorn and the Yellowstone for almost fifteen years and you will not regret my employment."

Ed followed Ashley into a well-appointed cabin. With an aura of supreme confidence, the businessman offered Ed a glass of port, but Ed declined.

"Nope General," said Ed, "I have sworn off of alcohol for good because I don't want to ever lose control of myself again. I thank you General for givin me this chance."

Ashley nodded admiringly, and then asked, "Can we rely upon the cooperation of the Arikara? I have been warned by Joshua Pilcher that they might close the river to white men any day now."

Ed thought about this news. "I have lived among them for years, yet I don't totally trust them. They are ornery, distrustful son-of-a-bitches and they just naturally don't like white men. They don't trust white traders because they took away their trade from the Shoshoni, Flathead, Crow and Nez Perce. Also white men have brought pox and measles among them on more than one occasion. However, the Arikara can be bribed with whiskey and the right trade goods."

Ashley said, "Mr. Rose, get your gear together and place it in my cabin. For the time being you will serve as my guide, interpreter and one of my hunters. See Jedediah Smith when you are ready to join us. We need fresh camp meat already because many young men have already joined up."

With that Ed boarded his canoe and went to gather the rest of his gear and possibles. He felt like the good times were returning. When the *Enterprise* left St. Louis, the Rocky Mountain Fur Company had already employed Jed Smith, Bill Sublette, Tom Fitzpatrick and over ninety other men. Ed rated a horse but he preferred to roam the bottoms and prairies ahead of the boat on foot so that he could track game. By the time the boat was paddled, pushed, pulled, polled and cordelled up the shallow river, he already had meat waiting at riverside camps. He provided meat fresh, smoked and jerked and had meat drying in strips each time the *Enterprise* came along side.

During the journey, Ed educated the other hunters about the natives on the prairie and the dangers of the mountains. He taught them about the Arikara, Mandan, Hidatsa and Assiniboine. He talked slowly but his words were vivid and precise, and full of assurance. He made the hunters rise before daylight to hunt their game and he cautioned them over and over about the habits of grizzly bears and how dangerous they could be.

When they neared the mouth of the Grand River, Ed told Ashley, "General, we are near the Rees and I suggest you double your lookouts and guards. I also suggest that tomorrow I lead you and some of your men to meet with Chief Grey Eyes."

At sunrise Ashley had several horses saddled. He directed Jed Smith, Bill Sublette and Tom Fitzpatrick to follow him and Ed to the Arikara villages. While they passed through fields of corn, pumpkins, beans and tobacco, in the distance they could see smoke rising from the smoke holes of the large dirt lodges.

Suddenly, some young men rode up in a cloud

of dust and began to whoop, "Ka'he! Ka'he! It is Five Scalps."

Ed raised his open palm toward them and spoke in Arikara. "Ride ahead of us and tell your chiefs that I am bringing white men to council and trade with them."

The young men whirled and raced back to the village, each wanting to be the first one to tell about the white traders. Ed led Ashley and his men on through the tall palisades and entered the lower village. A larger compound lay across the creek that separated the villages. Ed led his party on through a dark hallway and entered a large earth lodge, where logs supported the dome and pole fences separated the interior areas. In some areas there was hay, halters and gear for horses because they kept their horses inside during inclement weather.

In each lodge, areas were set aside for furs, for firewood, and for sleeping. A central fire pit emitted smoke through the hole in the roof, while tripod poles supported cookware, war equipment and personal belongings. In the back of the lodge, a hole in the floor led to an underground storage cellar that held dried meat, corn, tobacco and roots. Ladders were used to enter and leave the cellar.

Two head chiefs sat before a fire and one of them held a large ceremonial pipe. Ed turned to Ashley saying, "The big fellow is Little Soldier and the small, mean one is Grey Eyes. Watch out for the little one." He then raised his hand and greeted the chiefs before directing Ashley and his men to sit across the fire opposite them. After everyone was seated, Grey Eyes took four puffs from the pipe and then passed it on to Ed, who also took four puffs before passing it to Ashley. When everyone had smoked the pipe, Ed spoke slowly in Arikara.

"Oh great chiefs, these white men are trappers on their way to the Shining Mountains. They do not wish to rob you of your trade with your prairie neighbors. They only wish to be your friends and to purchase fifty horses from your people."

"They have two large boats on the river with many men and trade goods, and they wish to take their goods high into the mountains so they can trap and trade for furs. They are willing to give you fusils, lead, powder and arrow points in exchange for your horses."

The chiefs talked quietly among themselves before Grey Eyes asked Ed, "Will they also give guns to the Dakota, Teton, Cheyenne or Gros Ventre of the north?" Ed quickly replied, "No, my chiefs. These men will only use their weapons for protection against the Blood, Piegan and Blackfeet. They will not arm your enemies."

The chiefs again counseled quietly among themselves. Finally Grey Eyes said, "We will provide the white men with horses in exchange for guns and ammunition. Then I advise you to take them from here immediately. There are too many white men coming up the river and they always want our corn and horses while they trade us poor goods in return. They also use up our women and then they leave us their deadly diseases. Now go in peace, my friend."

Ed motioned to Ashley and his party that the council was over. Outside he told Ashley, "You have your horses but you have to give them some fusils, some lead and some powder. They will bring their animals to the river for exchange at sundown, and then we had better get the hell out of here."

General Ashley grasped Rose by the arm. "I will not forget your service to me, Rose. If you want a job with me, I will return down river soon and I will take you to St. Louis to help outfit my expedition for next year. I can always use a good man like you to help guide us over the Rockies."

Ed responded, "I will think on it General. I surely will think on it, because I'd love to see the Great Salt Lake and the Green River. I have heard so much about that area."

CHAPTER 19

When the party reached the mouth of the Yellowstone, they saw Major Henry's post on the right side of the Missouri River. The post was built of picket walls with two log blockhouses at opposite corners. The major and some of his tattered men met them when they beached the *Enterprise.*

General Ashley greeted his old partner. "Major, I see you have already built our fur post. It will do for a warehouse to store our plews and to hold our supplies. I have fifty fine horses for you at this time and I also have over a hundred new trappers."

Henry looked drawn but answered, "We sure need the horses and goods because, when you left us last fall, we were attacked by a large party of Assiniboine. We lost some of our supplies and fifty of our horses. I estimate that we have been damaged in the amount of $1,840 so far. We are also gettin mighty short of flour, coffee, hardtack and other essentials. We have only a few furs for you to take back to St. Louis because the Blackfeet have kept us runnin instead of trappin."

He continued, "Joshua Pilcher and his Missouri Fur Company have built a new post for the Crow at the mouth of the Bighorn. He is callin it Fort Benton. He is also sendin his partners, Robert Jones and Michael Immel, along with some trappers, up to the Three Forks of the Missouri."

Henry asked, "Should we send Rose to the Crow to try and disrupt their trade?"

"No," answered Ashley, "they will be limited on what the Crow can provide them, and I want you to beat them to the good trapping grounds near Three Forks. Send some of your men over to the Green River and the Snake River to find some rich beaver areas like you found before the war with the British. Those beaver fields should be fertile now, and we need to trap them before any more fur companies can reach these mountains."

Ashley concluded, "Clyman and I will take these furs and convert them to more supplies, then we will return here in the spring. I'll stop at the Arikara and hire Ed Rose to accompany me in St. Louis. I will need him more than ever in order to deal with the Arikara when we return. They were sure cantankerous during this trip, and they are beginning to worry me. I can always use Clyman as our hunter because of his experience. Get your goods unloaded Major and we will be on our way. By the way, Andrew, our expedition has been broadcast in the newspapers from New York to London, and if we are successful in our endeavor, we will both become famous."

When Ashley, Clyman and the boatmen sailed back to the Arikara villages, they anchored on a large sand spit and waited for Rose. Soon Ed came to their craft in a bullboat made from a large buffalo skin. It spun slowly from left to right as Ed stroked back and forth with his paddle. He finally landed it on the sand bar next to the *Enterprise.*

Ashley queried, "Have you decided, Rose. Are you joining my Rocky Mountain endeavor?"

"Yep," Ed responded, "I'm ready for a change a scenery. These Ree are spoilin for trouble and I don't want to have to decide who I'm fightin for."

Ed boarded the keelboat and the French boatmen shoved off. The boatmen were smelly and rowdy, but eager to get to the waterfront of St. Louis.

Ashley had more troubles financing his new supplies in St. Louis. His old creditors were reluctant to advance additional credit; therefore, he had to locate new sources, including selling many of his personal lands and mines. Once again he advertised in the newspapers for a hundred young men, but this time he offered them $200 in advance for two years. He signed up Hugh Glass, Milton Sublette, David Jackson and a young eighteen-year-old named James Bridger. He was leery of taking anyone so young into the mountains, but Bridger was a large, raw-boned lad and was the biggest braggart Ashley had ever heard. The trip might do him good.

Ashley then sent Ed Rose, Hugh Glass and James

Clyman to every bar and dive in St. Louis and St. Charles, looking for men to sober up and bribe into going to the mountains for two years. From those towns, they brought back the dregs of society.

During the winter Ashley spent a miserable time as the Lieutenant Governor presiding over the Missouri senate, and at the same time trying to finance his spring trapping campaign to the Yellowstone. During this time, Ed and Hugh Glass had plenty of opportunity to get to know each other better. While Ed was muscular and scarred from his earlier knife fight, Hugh was tall, wiry and unmarked. It was evident that the older man used his brain more than his brawn.

As they exchanged information, Ed said, "When I came to St. Louis I was hired by Manuel Lisa and Major Henry to go to the Bighorn River and build Fort Manuel to trade with the Crow. Me and Mr. Lisa had a big disagreement about how to win over the Indians and he fired me on the spot. I just stayed in the mountains with the Crow and became one of their war chiefs. I have been livin with the Crow and the Rees ever since. I reckon I have hired out as a guide and an interpreter to every expedition that has ever come up the Missouri."

Hugh offered, "Well I was educated in the East, captured by the pirate Jean Laffite, and finally recaptured on the prairie by the Loop Pawnee. This job is the best one I have had in twenty years."

Ed bragged, "Sure enough, I was a pirate with Pierre Laffite, the brother of Jean. I lived for a time down there in Barataria. We raided wrecked ships and some that hadn't even been wrecked yet. We took our loot to the *Vieux Carre'* in the old French town and spent it on the quadroons of Rampart Street."

"Har! Har!" squealed Glass. "Yep, I do remember them pretty quadroons and I also member Barataria. That's where Jean Laffite kidnapped me and held me aboard one of his ships. I was a captive for three years."

Glass chuckled, then added, "I was there when Laffite and Governor Claiborne had their big showdown. Claiborne offered a five hundred dollar reward for Laffite's head. Laffite then turned right around and offered fifteen hundred dollars for the governor's head. Jean and his brother set up a stolen goods business on Chartres Street at the Maspero's Exchange. They met and made deals right upstairs in plain sight."

"Things might have been disastrous if General Andy Jackson hadn't come to New Orleans in 1814 to whip the British. I was forced to man a cannon firin on the British as they came marchin up the Mississippi. We sure powdered the hell out of them. I jumped ship and fled upriver to Natchez-Under-the-Hill with Jackson's troops in order to get away from Laffite's clutches. I survived down on Silver Street in Natchez until I met some traders who had been among the Wolf Pawnee, or Pawnee Loop as the white traders call them."

Glass continued. "However, the Pawnee captured me before I could join up with them. They assigned me to a log-and-mud lodge that was about thirty-five feet in diameter. The walls were lined with sleepin bunks, while curtains separated the different families that lived in the lodge. I had several mothers who wanted to adopt me. The lodge had a central fire ring with a hole in the roof to allow smoke to vent. However, each family fixed their own meals and I had to practically go from one family to the other to get fed."

Ed laughed. "Well at least you didn't have to sleep with the horses in your lodge like I had to do when I lived with the Rees. By the way, I thought the Ree were tradin partners with the Pawnee."

Glass quickly responded, "They were but I never got to visit the Ree villages. Still, I know for a fact that my people went there to trade for vegetables, lead and powder. We traded them horses, pemmican, buffalo robes, meat and such."

Hugh went on, "I can tell you a story for the books, by God. When I lived with the Loops, back in 1820, I saw this here Indian Agent, Benjamin O'Fallon. I learned that he is the nephew of Governor William Clark and that old Clark raised him. Anyway, O'Fallon came to the Pawnee to make them sign some special peace treaty. Well, we had us a damn half-breed that liked to brag and try to be a big man. He began boastin about killin a prisoner during the Chicago Massacre of 1812 and while he was braggin he tried to rile the Pawnee against Mr. O'Fallon. Well, when O'Fallon heard bout it he just went and cut off this breeds' ears. He then gave him one hundred lashes with a whip and threw all the man's weapons into the Missouri. O'Fallon then forced the breed out on to the prairie and nobody has ever seen the man since."

Hugh continued telling his tales. "We had a flood that year up on the Missouri that plumb wiped out old Fort Atkinson. They had to totally rebuild the fort way up on the high bluff above the river."

Ed was surprised to hear this. "I have been to that fort many times and I can't believe it was flooded out. That bluff sure enough makes a nice ground to defend against hostiles, however, it don't have very good service from the river."

Ed considered what Hugh had told him about O'Fallon. Ed thought to himself, "I have done some pretty bad things in my day, but I would never have been that vicious, even to a hated enemy." He had never met O'Fallon but he had heard the man did not like Indians and that he dealt harshly with them.

Glass said, "I met William Becknell last year when he brought a mule train through Pawnee country on his way to Santa Fe and Taos. He opened a real nice trade over there but he had to run the gauntlet with the Comanches and Apaches. He informed me that the Red River was not navigable cause of giant logjams. However, he said that the Arkansas could be boated all the way to the Mississippi. He said he still preferred jumpin off the Missouri up at the new town of Franklin. He also told me about this here Rocky Mountain Fur Company and here I am."

Glass studied Ed. "You know," he said, "I can read and write and cipher real well. Can you read?"

Ed frowned. "Nope," he said, "I've been strugglin all

my life just to stay alive. I never learned readin or writin, but I reckon I know as much about the mountains and Indians as any man alive."

Glass nodded, "That's for sure, friend. That's for sure." From these simple exchanges the two became fast friends, and although they were complete opposites, they always seemed to have something to share and, sought each other's companionship.

Finally, on March 10, 1823 the *Rocky Mountains* and the *Yellowstone Packet* were loaded and began to sail their way up the Missouri River. Besides Rose and Glass, the party contained such luminaries as Jim Clyman, Tom Fitzpatrick, David Jackson, William Sublette, Milton Sublette, Black Harris, John Fitzgerald and Hiram Allen. Ashley was so excited that he hired musicians to entertain as the expedition sailed away, with colors flying. The party was still in sight of the city when the trailing boat ran aground and sprang a leak.

Soon after, a boatman fell overboard and drowned. When they reached St. Charles, they waited for a wagon carrying thirty kegs of gunpowder. However, a smoking driver ignited the wagon that carried the precious cargo. The gunpowder blew up, killing three men and their horses. Ashley had to immediately send a courier to the mines at Ste. Genevieve to arrange for more gunpowder. To finance the trip, Ashley and Henry had sold their lead and saltpeter mines. The potassium nitrate from the mines could have been used to make more gunpowder. Ashley sighed. He knew that if they had not sold their mines, they would not have had the capital for this new business. They could not afford both enterprises.

Ashley felt he could not wait for the powder to come from Ste. Genevieve, so he signed new notes of credit with Jacob and Samuel Hawken of St. Louis. They sent the new wagons loaded with thirty kegs of powder to meet the boats at the new town of Franklin, Missouri. Only God could stop Ashley now.

CHAPTER 20

When Ashley's party reached Franklin he was pleasantly surprised to see a celebration and parade in his honor.

The mayor said, "General Ashley, we owe you much, sir, for protecting our territory during the War of 1812. We had many Indian depredations instigated by the English until your militia chased them back into the wilderness. Tonight, we are holding a ball in your honor."

Ashley felt humbled. He said, "I thank you mayor. And I thank the good people of Franklin. I trust I will do you proud with my new expedition up the Missouri. I think your city will benefit financially from our trip."

When the boats reached Fort Atkinson at Council Bluffs several men from his boats enlisted in the Army. But several soldiers had been discharged and Ashley hired them as replacements. Ashley felt he got the better deal as the quality of his men improved.

In May Ed spotted Jed Smith paddling downstream. He called from the riverbank, "Smith, what are you doin down here on the Grand River?"

Smith called back, "I need to see the General. Major Henry sent me with a personal message. Where is Ashley?"

Ed ran down the bank as he called, "He is around the bend of the river cordellin his boat up stream. Just follow me." Ed ran almost as fast as Smith could paddle while they turned the curve of the river and saw the General's keelboat.

General Ashley recognized Jedediah. Ashley called, "Smith, what in tarnation are you doin here on the river?"

Jed hollered back, "General, we have been attacked by the Blackfeet and Major Henry is in dire need of more horses and supplies. "

Ashley directed, "Come aboard Jed so you can rest. We are near the Arikara and Rose thinks he can get us some more horses there. However, they have recently attacked Pilcher's Cedar Post and they appear hostile to all whites."

On May thirtieth, Ashley's party reached the great horseshoe bend of the Missouri below the Arikara villages. The Arikara had built a breastwork of cut timber on a large sandbar at the bend. The sandbar and the fortifications forced the river into a narrow channel, which placed any craft on the river into close contact with the Arikara villages. With this system, the Arikara had the river tightly guarded in front of their villages for over half a mile.

Ashley asked Ed, "Rose do you think you can still trade with the Ree?"

Ed answered, "I don't know General. If Pilcher has not punished them for attackin Cedar Post, they will be confident and difficult to work with."

"Damnation!" he exclaimed. "I won't let the red devils turn me back now. We need those horses one way or another. Men, load your guns and keep your powder dry."

He directed both keelboats to anchor in mid-channel. He then unloaded one skiff and said, "Rose, you go over to the villages and see if you can get a meeting for me with their head chiefs. I need those horses."

While Ed was gone, Ashley and Smith took some trade goods and set up a treaty camp on the beach near the river. At the same time he ordered both boats to load their swivel guns and have gunners at the ready in case things went wrong.

Ed went to the lower village and brought Grey Eyes and Little Soldier to the beach camp to meet Ashley. The chiefs held their heads proudly aloft as they waddled from the lower village to Ashley's campsite. Ashley offered them small gifts while Ed spoke, "Chiefs, my great leader wishes once again to trade for ponies. He needs fifty animals to cross to the Shining Mountains. He is an honorable man and his words are true. Will you come with us to his large wooden boat to council?"

Little Soldier solemnly shook his head to mean 'no', but the unpredictable Grey Eyes agreed and entered the skiff. They rowed slowly back to the *Rocky Mountains* keelboat while Ed continued to reassure Grey Eyes of their intentions.

While they were boarding the larger boat, Ed explained to Ashley, "Chief Grey Eyes lost a son during the raid on Cedar Post. He is bitter and still grieving." In the meantime, Grey Eyes was carefully scanning the boat to examine the men and their weapons. The swivel gun especially fascinated him, but he did not clearly understand its firepower.

Ashley said to Ed, "Offer him anything except guns, but get us forty or fifty horses. Henry is in dire need at once."

Ed spoke to Grey Eyes, "Chief, my leader wishes to once again trade with you for fifty horses. His partner has been robbed by the Assiniboine and he needs these animals to get to the Shining Mountains so they can trap beaver and not interfere with your river trade."

Grey Eyes offered, "The white men build trading posts on our river and they take away our trade with the other nations. We are angry with the white-eyes."

Ed responded in Arikara, "General Ashley is in competition with the white man Pilcher and his Cedar Post. The General's men follow the beaver up to the mountain streams and he does not build trading posts in your country."

Grey Eyes responded, "But the white men sell guns to the Teton and the Dakota so they can kill and rob us, yet, you say that the white chief will not trade us guns. Why should we trust the white men?"

Ed offered one last thought on the subject, "General Ashley traded you fusils last season but he will not provide anymore guns to you or any of the other tribes because tribesmen are using them to kill his men. He is afraid that the good tribes will trade guns to the bad tribes and the General has many enemies, including the Pecunies and Bloods."

In conclusion, Chief Grey Eyes turned to Ed and said, "Five Scalps, you have always fought well and you have been loyal to the Arikara. I believe your words of peace, but I must talk with my other chiefs and counselors. Have your white chief stay one more sun and I will let you know of our decision."

When they boarded the skiff to leave, Grey Eyes again carefully scanned the two keelboats. Ed brought some trade goods into the skiff that he wanted to give the chief when they went ashore. He still hoped to influence Grey Eyes when he met with the other chiefs.

In the meantime, Ashley decided to keep his two keelboats anchored in the middle of the river for safety. The General waited all day before Ed took word to him that the chiefs would meet the next morning to consummate the trade for horses.

Ashley and his men spent another nervous night and established double watches of guard duty on both keelboats. At daybreak Ashley began to ferry his trade goods to the beach with his remaining skiffs. Everything was laid out on blankets and Grey Eyes, Little Soldier and the council sat down facing the trade goods. After smoking the peace pipe, slow deliberations began. Ed was able to trade some of the goods for twenty horses from Little Soldier's band before negotiations hit a snag.

Grey Eyes then spoke. "We want fifty guns, lead and black powder."

When Ed explained this to Ashley, the General yelled, "Hell no!" The General then pointed to the knives, arrow points and cloth, but Grey Eyes slowly and firmly shook his head in the negative.

Finally the General turned to Ed. "Rose," he said, "we can't spare any of our guns or any of our powder. Find another way to get us out of here gracefully and perhaps we can trade with the Mandan or the Hidatsa up stream."

Ed talked long and calmly with Grey Eyes and the other chiefs, but he did not make much headway. Ashley still wanted to try to trade for more horses the next day. He told Smith to hobble the horses they had already obtained. He ordered them held on the beach and set up guards to keep them guarded until morning. The General then took all the trade goods and other items back to the keelboats and set up two-hour watches among the boatmen. Ed stayed with the chiefs and counseled into the night. During the night, headwinds on the river increased to gale force. The boats had to remain anchored while the men and the new horses were exposed on the beach forty yards away.

At morning light, Ed returned to Ashley. "General," he said, "I have talked to Little Soldier and he fears that Grey Eyes intends to attack us before we leave his village. Chief Bear in the upper village wishes to council with you, but he does not want to leave his lodge. He requests that you visit him there."

"Can he get me horses?" asked Ashley.

Ed frowned, "I don't know, sir. He is a mild chief but I don't rightly know if he carries much weight in his village. It might even be a trap to try to divide our forces."

Ashley swore, "Well by God, I won't go then. We'll stay put and double our guard until I can get my men and horses off their damn beach." He then began directing his men to set up a defensive position. The commotion of their activities and preparation could be heard up and down the river.

"Smith, strengthen the night guard," Ashley commanded, "Keep only about fifteen men on shore. Rose, you stay there in the villages and keep your ears to the ground. Let me know at once if you detect any mischief. We have to find a way to sail out of here in the morning, more horses or not."

Smith replied, "Aye, General I will post the duty list." With that he quickly turned to the task Ashley had given him. Men on the beach began digging rifle pits and moved their horses farther along the riverbank for their protection. When the wind finally calmed, the air became so quiet that the men could hear the water as it eddied around snags and limbs sticking up from the river bottom. They could hear the breathing of their colleagues and the thump of their own heartbeats as their pulses rose with each new release of adrenaline.

That night a discharged soldier from Fort Atkinson,

named Aaron Stephens, entered the village and asked for Ed. He said, "Rose, I ain't been with a woman for at least three years and I'll trade you my army rifle if you can get me a squaw tonight before we leave this village. I might not have another chance, so can you do it?"

Ed knew better, but he could not turn down a trade for a good army rifle, so he told Stephens, "Follow me. I will show you a real smart Ree woman. She is young and as pert a gal as you have ever seen this side of St. Louis. I have some trade beads and some vermilion that you can offer her."

Ed almost smiled as he led Stephens toward the second village. He had not seen his Ree squaw since last fall and he sure would like to see her before they left. She had a sister that was tolerable to look at and was always eager to trade herself for beads or cloth. Ed hungered for some companionship as much as the young man did. Stephens could hardly contain his enthusiasm as he and Ed crossed the creek between the two villages.

Ed cautioned him, "Stay with me now and don't speak. We must pretend we are just two Ree braves goin for a stroll. Come on now." There was very little moonlight this evening and the wind was blowing as they passed through an Arikara cornfield. They came to the second set of palisades and entered the village. Ed led Stephens quietly around the outside of the earthen lodges until he came to the lodge of his former father-in-law.

When they entered, Ed called softly, "Rabbit Woman! Rabbit Woman! It is I, Five Scalps. I have returned to you." He began to feel in the area where he remembered where her sleeping robes to be. Suddenly, a small hand grasped his arms and a woman's soft flesh pressed against his hard body. But before Ed could caress his lover, he was viciously attacked.

Ed could not determine who his attacker was in the dim light of the lodge fire, but he shoved Rabbit Woman aside, grabbed his Green River knife and yelled, "Get the hell out of here, Stephens! Run for your life! Return to the boat for help! It's every man for himself."

Ed fought clear of his attacker and dashed out of the lodge right behind Stephens. However, Ree braves were slashing with their knives as the two men fled. Ed saw Stephens fall to the ground as his attackers continued to slash him while he struggled to get to his feet. The man had no opportunity to defend himself.

Ed ran on and fled around the lodges and through a hole in the pickets. He stopped only long enough to see if he was still being pursued, but apparently the attackers were concentrating on his hapless white comrade. The only thing Ed could hear now was his fluttering heart and his wheezing breath. He continued to sprint through the cornfield and across the shallow creek to the lower village.

He continued through the lower village before he could see that he had a clear run to the camps on the beach. He yelled, "Halloo! It is I, Rose! Hold your fire, men! It's me, Rose! Call the men to arms! The Rees have killed Stephens! They have massacred him!"

Ashley, a light sleeper, heard scraping on the deck of his boat. He loaded two of his pistols and slowly opened his cabin door. In the moonlight he saw three Ree braves and fired his weapons. Although he surely did not hit them, they dove in the river and swam for the upper shore. At nearly the same time, he saw Rose and his men running about on the beach. Frantically, Ed yelled to Ashley.

"General," he yelled, "they have killed Stephens. I have been warned to get out of here before the Ree attack. We need to get our men off of the beach as fast as we can." The sky started to rain Ree arrows and musket balls. Clouds of smoke rose from the pickets and fortifications as gunpowder exploded from their British-made muskets.

Ashley began to bark orders. "Pull up the anchors! Move the boats down river! Send skiffs to our men on the beach! Tell the men to swim their horses to safety!"

The French voyageurs panicked and did nothing. Finally Glass took a skiff to the shore to try to direct the men staying with Jed Smith. Two army friends of Stephens yelled, "We ain't leavin until we get the body of Stephens!"

Ed yelled at them, "His eyes have been gouged out, his head has been cut off and his body has been mutilated. Forget him and save yourself. Get those horses off the beach, fast!"

Clyman began to yell, "General, send the boats. General, send the boats, quick!"

However, Ashley was too busy trying to get the French voyageurs to save the keelboats. He yelled, "Weigh the anchors, scum! Weigh all anchors, damn you!"

He aimed his big pistol at one large Creole and demanded, "Raise that damned anchor or I shall kill you here and now!"

The big sailor feared the General more than he feared the Arikara and finally pulled the anchors up. The boatmen on the other boat had to cut their anchor ropes. Ashley continued to yell orders, "Set those skiffs ashore for our men. Move them now!"

One large skiff was sent, but the smaller one was already on the beach where Stephens had left it. The boatmen made it to the beach and loaded some of the frantic men, but as they tried to return to the keelboat, two of the paddlers were shot and fell into the river current. The trappers did their best to try to get to the drifting keelboat.

Several men and horses fell under the first Arikara fusillade. Some of the men fired back but they could not see their targets behind the pickets. Some of the Arikara left their fortifications and advanced toward the men remaining on the beach. Clyman, Smith and Glass defended the evacuation as Ed and George Yount grabbed the few horses that had not already been killed and raced down the river bottom as fast as they could. Glass was shot in the leg before he could get out of rifle range, but he still grabbed all of his weapons before he jumped into the river.

Weighted down with his pistols and bullets, and with the powder horn he carried in a leather pouch around his neck, Glass swam toward the nearest keelboat. He held his rifle, old Betsy, high above the water as he struggled in the stream. The current carried him past the boat but Reed Gibson reached out and grabbed the barrel of his rifle. As he was pulled aboard the boat, Hugh's buckskin suit began to seep water like a sieve. He turned to thank Gibson, but stared in disbelief as an Arikara bullet pierced his friend's chest, killing him instantly. All Hugh could do was take cover and tend to his own wounds. Poor Gibson had gone under.

In the meantime, one twenty-man skiff and one ten-man skiff arrived to assist the remaining men stranded on the beach, but several of the boatmen were also wounded. Some of the men simply jumped into the river even though they could not swim because there was no more room in the boats. Total chaos reigned.

CHAPTER 21

Only the distance from the main barricades prevented total annihilation. Those who had not dug pits hid behind fallen horses. As the two keelboats drifted in the current around the bend, Ashley slowly began to regain order on his boats.

When they reached a timbered island he had the boats put ashore and ordered that log defenses be built. He feared that the Ree warriors might pursue them on horseback. The men began to arrive in small groups – some were wounded and barely able to walk. Most had lost their guns or other weapons. Ed and Yount rode in with a few remaining horses, which they hobbled on the island to help protect them from further depredation by the Arikara.

The General began to take inventory of his missing men and supplies. "Men," he said, "I want you to rearm yourselves because we are going to charge up the river and pass those heathen compounds. We have to get on with the trapping season or I'll go broke."

The broken and frightened men began to grumble and wail. They cursed the general and cried almost in unison, "We didn't sign on to fight no damn Injun war an get killed or scalped." Even though they had been paid two years in advance, many threatened to desert on the spot.

Smith offered, "General, I think we need to send runners to Fort Atkinson to ask for Army help. I can also send a runner to Major Henry to ask him to come at once to our assistance." Ashley weighed his options but did not feel secure about any of them. He owed too much money to give up now and return to St. Louis. He decided to take Smith's advice. He learned that twelve of his men had been killed outright and many were still missing. Even some of the eleven wounded might yet die.

On the morning of the third of June, Ashley decided on a plan of action. He moved the camp twenty-five miles downstream below the Moreau River. He then sent Smith to get aid from Henry. Further, he sent a letter down to Indian Agent Benjamin O'Fallon. He also sent a letter to Colonel Henry Leavenworth at Fort Atkinson to request troops to punish the Arikara. He sent another letter to Edward Charles, his old friend and editor of the *Missouri Republican* newspaper, informing him of his predicament and the attack by the Arikara. He also informed the readers that if any company planned on ascending the river they should be well armed and carry at least one six-pound cannon for their protection.

He then loaded the wounded aboard the *Yellowstone Packet* with all the goods he could not get on the *Enterprise* and *Rocky Mountains*. He ordered that all his extra supplies were to be put off and stored at Fort Kiowa, which was controlled by the French Fur Company.

Ed and the other hunters had to go ashore to obtain camp meat for the company. But after one month, game became scarce and still no reinforcements had arrived. The hunters were so spooked that only Ed, Clyman and old Glass were brave enough to go afar to find game.

Finally in July Smith brought in Major Henry and fifty valuable men. Henry reported to his partner, "General, we have had a poor showing in the mountains this season. The Blackfeet have killed four of my men and they had to abandon over two hundred good traps. I have only a few packs of fur to show for my efforts. I had to leave twenty men behind to guard our supplies at Fort Henry."

Ashley could hardly believe his ears. It seemed that no matter how hard they tried, everything seemed against them. What else could possibly happen? Last year they lost a keelboat with all of their supplies and goods. This year their shipment of guns and powder blew up before it even reached the boats. Now he had lost half of his men, all of his horses, and many of his supplies to the damn Arikara.

He told Henry, "Well Major, I have had at least fifteen men killed and a large number of deserters. I only have about twenty-five able-bodied men left here. If we don't get army troops here soon, we will lose the entire beaver season. We must descend the river until we can get help."

With that they dropped down to the mouth of the Teton River, where they found a Sioux camp. However, the Sioux had no spare horses. Ashley left Henry in charge while he descended to Fort Kiowa. While there he received a letter on the nineteenth of July from O'Fallon informing him that Colonel Leavenworth would lead a full-scale military expedition against the Arikara.

As Indian Agent, O'Fallon was concerned because the Blackfeet had killed seven members of the Missouri Fur Company and Major Henry had lost four men to the Blackfeet. He had to put a stop to the Indian depredations immediately, because it was hurting American fur interests and American claims to the Northwest. Furthermore, the Hudson Bay Company was promoting British control of the Rocky Mountains and the Columbia River Country. British influence had been causing bad blood between the natives and the American trappers since 1812.

Colonel Leavenworth left Fort Atkinson on the twenty-second of June with two hundred thirty officers and men. He also brought three keelboats and two six-pound cannons.

O'Fallon recruited Joshua Pilcher and sixty of his trappers. Further, Pilcher was able to shame and recruit forty-three of Ashley's deserters to join the expedition. O'Fallon sent a letter with Pilcher appointing Major Henry to the post of Sub Indian Agent for the Upper Missouri. When Ashley learned that the "Missouri Legion" was ascending the river, he returned to his men.

CHAPTER 22

Leavenworth commandeered Ashley's keelboat, the *Yellowstone Packet,* for the expedition. But while the flotilla was ascending the Missouri, one of Leavenworth's boats sank, losing seven men along with their guns and supplies. However, Pilcher was able to recruit seven hundred mounted Sioux warriors who wanted to help punish the Arikara.

After traveling for five weeks, Leavenworth and his expedition reached Ashley at the mouth of the Cheyenne River on the thirteenth of July. Leavenworth immediately began to organize his 'Legion'.

He divided the Rocky Mountain Fur Company into two companies, one under General Ashley and the other under Major Henry. Both men were already officers in the Missouri Militia. He appointed Jed Smith and Hiram Scott as captains while others became lieutenants, ensigns, quartermasters and sergeant majors. Pilcher's men were organized into a rifle company with Angus

McDonald named a captain and placed in charge of the Sioux mounted auxiliary. The Legion reached the Grand River on the ninth of August and Leavenworth directed the Sioux to attack the Arikara while his men surrounded both villages.

Ed Rose became an ensign and was assigned as interpreter and messenger between the Legion and the Arikara villages while the Arikara warriors fought the Sioux in the cornfields.

Leavenworth could not attack because he could not tell the difference between the Sioux and the Arikara. By the time he finally decided on an action, the warriors had barricaded themselves in their villages and had turned defiant again. Because his cannons were still down river, Leavenworth decided to halt military actions until the next morning, when he sent Ed into the villages to assess the strength of the Arikara.

Meanwhile, the Sioux began to roast fresh corn from the Arikara cornfields. The odor of dead horses and dead bodies and roasted corn permeated the still night air. Many of the white 'legionnaires' sat around campfires drinking whiskey, waiting for the ensuing battle.

When the sun rose over the Missouri, Leavenworth unlimbered his six-pound cannons and started pounding the two villages with cannonballs. Most of the shells fell ineffectively into the fifteen-foot wooden pickets. By noon he halted the artillery and began a rifle assault. He assigned Pilcher the upper village and Ashley the lower village. By afternoon he called off the entire assault.

Pilcher screamed, "Colonel, what in hell are you

doing? We have the bastards! Don't quit on them now, for god's sake!"

Ed Rose came running from the lower village in a zigzag line as he ducked sniper bullets. He gasped, "Colonel, you have done a lot a damage in there. There are dead Ree everywhere and Grey Eyes and the other chiefs are weakening."

Leavenworth seemed dazed and confused. He meekly offered, "I'm afraid I'll lose too many men against their fortifications. The only way I can win is by total annihilation. If I did that there would be hell to pay in Washington. I can't afford a bloodbath." He seemed to lose all confidence when his guns could not breach the wooden barricades.

Pilcher became enraged. "You're a damn coward, Colonel. If we don't punish these heathens now, every damn tribe on the Missouri River will know we ain't no better than buffalo shit. Hellfire, I'll whip them with my own men."

Leavenworth winced from the scolding, but he held his resolve. He turned to his own officers, "Have your men fall back and regroup, then report to my tent." He turned to Pilcher and said, "Sir, I am directing you and General Ashley to keep the Arikara penned down in their villages until morning. I'm going to my tent to develop a new battle plan." Ed was as disgusted as Pilcher was. He had seen first hand how badly the Ree had been pounded and knew they were ready to surrender with a little push.

Ed went to Ashley's camp to give him his report.

"Sir," he told Ashley, "I don't know how long they will allow me to run back and forth between their villages before they consider me their enemy. We need to get this thing over in a hurry or they'll get brazen again."

Ashley retreated to his tent in disgust. The Sioux began raiding the Arikara cornfields again, taking bags of fresh roasting ears. After they loaded their horses, they began drifting away in twos and threes, heading back to their villages. The Sioux had lost interest in the white man's method of fighting.

That night Ed made another foray into the villages. He found Chief Little Soldier, who warned him, "The white men have killed Chief Grey Eyes. I ask you to leave our lodges and protect yourself as best you can. Many of our younger chiefs call you a traitor."

Ed ran back through the gap in the pickets and reported directly to Ashley instead of going through Leavenworth. "General," he offered, "we have killed Grey Eyes. The chiefs are in council and they are almost ready to surrender."

Ashley gleamed, "Splendid Rose. Return to them immediately and assure them that if they surrender to me, I will protect them and their property. I only want my horses and restitution for my losses."

Ed knew that Ashley was primarily concerned with his investment, but the man would honor his word. Ed eventually brought Little Soldier, Bear and other minor chiefs to a neutral campfire outside the Arikara compound. The natives sat on their robes as they smoked and awaited Pilcher and Leavenworth. When they arrived, the Colonel told Ed what to say.

"Tell the Ree chiefs the white father in Washington is unhappy with his Arikara children for attacking his white children on the river that belongs to all of them. Tell them to restore any property they have taken from General Ashley and to replace the horses he has lost."

Before Ed could interpret the Colonel's words to the chiefs, Pilcher began to berate Leavenworth. "What about my property that they destroyed at Cedar Post," he said. "Between the Rees and the Blackfeet, I have been practically wiped out of business. Those damn Blood Indians killed my partners, Jones and Immel, and they stole over fifteen thousand dollars worth of my pelts. They even burned Fort Bent and its contents clear to the ground. I want some justice too by God or I'm gonna take things into my own hands."

Ed interrupted. "The chiefs say they will return what they have, but our big guns have killed most of the horses and have destroyed many of the goods. We have also killed many of their women and children. However, they promise future peace on the river in spite of their losses."

Leavenworth weighed Rose's words. There was really nothing left that he could do. To go on further would be futile, so he replied, "Ask the chiefs to smoke the peace pipe with us to show their sincerity and then we will leave them in peace."

While the peace pipe was passed around, Pilcher arose almost speechless. He screamed, "I'll be damned if I will be a party to this farce. I will protest to Superintendent Clark, to General Atkinson and to Senator Calhoun. Colonel, you have not heard the last of me in this regard." With that he stormed out of the meeting. The chiefs seemed very much disturbed and suddenly Leavenworth had his men try to arrest some of them to hold them hostage until a treaty could be drawn up.

Scuffling broke out and shots were fired as the chiefs broke and ran for the barricades of their village. In turn, Ashley and Leavenworth fled back to their respective compounds for their own safety. Ed followed, listening to Ashley curse. "That damned incompetent imbecile. How in tarnation did Leavenworth ever become an officer in the regular army? I would not allow him in our own Missouri Militia. Now I agree with Pilcher, that colonel is a total coward."

Leavenworth stayed up all night drafting a treaty. He was in denial regarding the disastrous campaign he was conducting. In his paranoia, he feared that the Sioux might join with the Arikara in their war against him.

When the sun rose over the river, Ed again came running from the lower village. He yelled to Ashley, "General, they have gone. All of them fled during the night. I can only find three rifles, one horse and a few robes. They only left the old mother of Chief Grey Eyes. She is alone and blind."

When Leavenworth arrived with his treaty, there was nothing left. He told Ashley, "General, you may now proceed with your trapping enterprise. I will file my report with Washington and General Atkinson. When you can take inventory you can provide me with the amount of your losses. I will see what I can get out of the government for you." Ashley hurried to reorganize his boats, men and supplies. He was still short of horses but he would just have to do with what he had or he would lose the entire trapping season.

Ed muttered, "Well I reckon I can forget ever goin back to the Rees. With old Grey Eyes dead, I don't think Little Soldier is strong enough to protect me from the young bucks who think I have betrayed them."

After Leavenworth and Ashley and their men departed, Pilcher ordered, "Gordon, keep McDonald back with you and burn them damn villages and their crops to the ground. I don't want the Ree to ever forget Joshua Pilcher and the Missouri Fur Company."

As the flotillas descended the river, big clouds of smoke billowed up on the horizon. Ed knew immediately what was happening and he rushed to get Ashley from his cabin. The General looked at the smoke in horror.

"That damn Pilcher," said Ashley. "He has put his foot in it now. It will be some time before we can ever ascend the river again. We had better just plan overland trips from now on."

Ed knew that his own fate was sealed also. He could never go back to the Arikara, because they would never forgive him for his role in the war with the white eyes.

CHAPTER 23

Ashley sent Major Henry and thirty men, along with only six horses, to get their furs and supplies and to close Fort Henry on the Yellowstone. The remainder of the crew floated on or followed the *Rocky Mountains* down river back to Fort Kiowa, which they reached in September.

Ashley could only acquire enough horses for eleven men. He said, "Smith I'm sending you and Rose with a trapping party to locate the Crow. I want you to winter with them, then cross the Rockies to the Green River next spring. I'll meet you there in June with new supplies."

Smith put Ed out front of the brigade to keep them on the trail and to find friendly tribes to trade for more horses. Included in the party were James Clyman, Bill Sublette, Tom Fitzpatrick, Tom Eddie, Arthur Branch, Tom Stone, Bill Williams and Tom Black. They ascended the White River in good spirits; however, as they entered the Badlands, they went without water for two days before Ed finally located an old waterhole.

169

Smith ordered, "Rose, push on ahead and try to get us adequate water. Some of the men are becoming ill and are dehydrated." Ed knew Smith was an educated young man and very smart, but he knew from experience that the men were also getting too much alkali and heavy minerals into their systems. They needed fresh buffalo meat to replenish their energy.

Ed told Smith, "Captain, I'll leave rock pyramids along the trail to mark my way. If I run out of rocks, I'll use buffalo dung piled up high. If there is danger, I'll make a cross by the trail." When Ed finally located good water, he fired his rifle three times. Slowly, the men started straggling into camp by twos and threes. By dark all the men had come to camp except Frances Branch and David Stone.

Since Ed was in the best condition, he volunteered to look for the missing men. "Captain, I'll take some water and go for the last two men. I'll be back by morning." At midnight, Ed slowly rode into camp with the two worn out men. The entire party rested for two days before again proceeding to the Cheyenne and up to the Black Hills. Instead of skirting the hills, Smith led his party into a narrow valley, searching for beaver as they went. They struggled along until they ran out of forage for their horses. Five of the mounts became so weak that Smith left them behind with Thomas Eddie, Frances Branch and Poe Williams so they could recover before they were brought forward.

Smith directed, "Men, rest the horses and then come along when they are well enough to move. You can follow our main trail since we will stop from time to time to trap for beaver. Rose will go in search of the Crow to acquire fresh mounts. We will need them if we are to reach the Bighorn before winter."

Ed called out, "Just follow my rock markins. The top rock will point you to the right trail."

After five days of travel, Smith and his men were struggling through a brushy bottom on foot while they were leading their mounts. Suddenly, a large, grey-backed grizzly charged from the bottom and grabbed Smith before he could react. Smith jabbed his Green River knife into its breast, breaking the blade at the hilt. This made the bear even more aggressive. The bear grabbed Smith's head with its mouth and began to sling him about. Each of Smith's men tried to line up for a shot but they feared hitting their leader. Blood was spurting from the bear as it made one last sling of Smith's body, casting him more than ten feet into the brush.

Now that Smith was clear, Tom Black fired his sixty-caliber Hawken into the bear's head, killing it instantly. "Good God!" exclaimed Clyman. "That grizzly has killed the Captain. He has chewed his head damn near off. Help me quick!"

Several men ran to extract Smith from the bushes. He had blood all over him. They could not immediately tell which blood belonged to the bear and which belonged to their leader. Smith was in great pain, but he could hear his men talking about the seriousness of his wounds.

He urged them, "Sew me up boys. I'll be fine if someone will just sew me up."

They all backed away except Clyman. He said, "Hell Captain, I don't know nothin about doctorin humans. I've only sewed up horses, my shirts and my trousers."

Smith thought he was going to pass out, but he offered reassurance to Clyman. "Jim, just do the best you can. You will find a needle, thread and scissors in my possible bag on my horse. Tom, you and Bill locate fresh water for a campsite. I think we need to rest here for a spell until I am able to travel."

Clyman used his water pouch to wash and clean Smith's bloody hair. His scalp was ripped open to the bone in several places. As he cleaned the drying blood away, he noticed that most of Smith's right ear was barely hanging from the side of his head.

He sewed the wounds together as good as he could, and then he tried to secure what was left of Smith's ear to his head. Smith would never look normal again, but he would recover. The men made a litter to carry their leader until they located a new campsite. It took ten days before Smith was well enough to travel again. When the brigade finally moved on, they traveled west until they reached the Belle Fourche River, where they located a friendly band of Cheyenne hunters. While camped and eating fresh buffalo ribs, a party of white men rode in with Smith's three stranded men and their refreshed horses.

"I'm Charles Kemmle," offered the bearded leader. "This here is Bill Gordon. We're with the Missouri Fur Company. We found your boys back there in the Black Hills. They were all tuckered out. They told us where you all were bound and here we are. Our boss, Josh Pilcher, sent us to winter with the Crow. Can we travel with you boys for a while?"

Smith still had bandages all around his head but he managed a smile. "We welcome the company of you fellows," he said. "I have sent a man on ahead to locate the Crow and procure new horses. As you can see I have been in a fight with a grey-backed bear. I don't know for sure which one of us is in the worst condition, except we have eaten most of the bear, and we have his hide staked out to be cured for a robe."

They talked into the night sharing information. At sunup the newly constituted party proceeded across the rolling prairie. It took two days to reach the Powder River. As they traveled, they continued to follow the stone communiqués left by Ed. Near the southeast bank they found a pile of stones with a round one on top. Here they setup camp and waited. On the second day they saw Ed coming along the sloping bank of the stream.

He had a dozen native warriors with him. As they rode up, Ed said, "I found these Crow hunters and they were able to get us some spare horses. They'll lead us to Chief Long Hair's village. The Mountain Crow are on the Wind River and the River Crow are on the Bighorn River at the mouth of the Greybull River. Which village do you want to join up with, Captain?"

Smith consulted with Keemle and Gordon. "We'll join up with the Mountain Crow in the Wind River Valley," he told Ed. "When spring comes we will be closer to the mountain passes that lead to the Green River."

The next day Ed led them over the southern tip of the Bighorn Mountains and descended Poison Creek to the Wind River. They followed the Little Wind to the area north of White Horse Draw and met the first lodges of the Mountain Crow. Smith located John Weber's brigade and rode up to them eagerly. All the men dismounted to shake hands all around and to exchange tales about their respective ordeals. Chief Long Hair invited the white trapper leaders to his council fire. Ed waited patiently as Long Hair's chiefs passed the peace pipe around.

Finally, Ed said, "Chief, these men wish to winter with your people. During the green-grass season Captain Smith and Captain Weber wish to take their men over the passes to the Seeds-ka-dee, but Captain Keemle and Captain Gordon wish to stay in Absaroka so they can trap your streams. Will your people feed and protect them?"

Long Hair paused for some time before replying. "The white men are our friends. If they put their trust in the Sparrowhawk people, we will not betray them. If they cheat us, my people will rob them to get even. Because of our friend, Five Scalps, we will trust your word."

He then addressed Ed directly. "My son, will you go to the Seeds-ka-dee with the white men?"

"No, my beloved chief," said Ed. "When the weather clears I will visit my relatives among the River Sparrow-hawk people on the Greybull."

Long Hair nodded, then directed his herald, "Antelope's Heart, ride among our people and announce the intentions of Five Scalps and the white men. Explain that I have decreed that we will provide them with lodging and with food, and that we will protect our new guests from enemies until the green grass grows again in Absaroka."

The council then broke up and the members went their separate ways. Ed went to locate his own lodge so he could wait out the early storms of the season. The remainder of the trapping parties began to set up their own lodges and camps while native maidens eyed the new visitors.

CHAPTER 24

Major Henry took his thirteen men aboard the *Rocky Mountains* keelboat and headed upriver toward Fort Henry, which stood at the junction of the Yellowstone and the Missouri Rivers. The men in the boat included Hugh Glass, who had been wounded by the Arikara, John Fitzgerald, James Bridger, George C. Yount, Edmund Flagg, Moses "Black" Harris, August Neill, James Anderson, Orange Clark, George Harris, St. George Cooke, William Allen, and James Hall.

When they reached the mouth of the Grand River, Henry beached his craft and joined his seven mounted trappers on the shore. He led his party up the Grand toward Yellowstone country. As they progressed, Glass, Harris and Allen served as hunters. All of the men were experienced at hunting, but Glass continually went off on his own track, without regard to the other hunters and the brigade.

Glass had been cautioned numerous times to stay

closer to the party, and to keep a sharp eye for hostile natives and white bears. He was also warned that grizzly females were roaming with their cubs at this time of year, foraging for food. Hugh ignored the cautions of the others. Since he had lived among the Pawnee for several years, he feared none of the natives. And as long as he had his precious Hawken rifle, Betsy, he feared no bears.

One day the hunters came upon a large thicket of plums, and Hugh followed a narrow trail through the bushes. While he proceeded through the thicket with his cocked rifle, he was viciously grabbed by huge white teeth and was flung into the air. The giant teeth bit into his throat and into his skull while long talons slashed his arms, legs and back. At last, the mother bear released Glass and went to check on her cubs.

Needless to say, Hugh was in shock. He was unable to run or climb a tree to escape another attack if she came back. He could barely lift his rifle when the crazed bear returned and attacked him again. This time, however, Hugh fired old 'Betsy' into the bear's breast at point blank range. The close proximity of the blast set the grizzly's fur on fire. Unfortunately, the large bullet just seemed to make the bear angrier. Resuming her vicious attack, she bit and tore at Hugh's body. When she threw Hugh through the air, she started to bleed profusely from her wound. Once again she left Glass and trotted back into the thicket to locate her cubs.

During this second attack, no one in the party had been able to fire at the bear for fear of hitting Glass. One of the fat cubs even chased Black Harris into the stream before he regained his composure and blew the small bear apart with his large bore rifle.

Several of the men then raced to Hugh to tend to his wounds, but he was torn so badly that no one knew where to begin to sew him up. They took pieces of their dirty clothes and began to tie up some of the more serious wounds in his arms and legs. They even swathed his bloody head in bandages so they would not have to look at the white bone that showed through his flesh. Air bubbles escaped from Hugh's neck and back where the bear's talons had pierced his lungs. Some of the men went looking for the grizzly. They found that the bear had bled to death from the large ball discharged into her breast from Hugh's rifle.

Major Henry rode up and instructed some of the men to set up a camp to take care of Glass. He ordered, "Potts, you and Yount get some straight poles and make a litter in order to carry Glass until he passes away."

Although it seemed obvious to everyone that Glass could not live long, the men carried him for several days while Glass moaned and cried from the exertion. The injured man fell in and out of consciousness from the pain and the loss of blood. Henry finally made a camp by a spring in a clump of willows, where there was good shade and water.

Henry spoke to his men. "I need two volunteers to stay with Glass until he goes under. I will pay ten dollars per day for anyone who will take care of him and give him a proper burial. Do I have any takers?" Because John Fitzgerald had recently been discharged from the

Army, he desperately needed the money. John stepped forward.

"Major," Fitzgerald said, "I will stay with him. I know Glass pretty well and he is a fine fellow. I know he would do the same for me."

After a pause, young Jim Bridger spoke up. "Major, I need money to send back to my family, so I'll stick it out with Mr. Fitzgerald and I'll do my duty."

Henry said, "Thank you, boys. Our brigade needs to get back on the trail so we can get to Fort Henry before the first snow. When Glass passes away, you boys bury him proper, and then catch up with us. We will leave tree markers and rock piles so you can follow our trail. You will be paid in credit at Fort Henry when you arrive." Major Henry did not mention the Blackfeet or the marauding Arikara who were in the country around them. But everyone knew of the danger traveling through this country.

After the brigade departed, Fitzgerald and Bridger started worrying about renegades and more bears. Every sound of the wilderness drove stakes through their hearts. At last, Fitzgerald began psychological warfare on young Bridger.

"Boy," said Fitzgerald, "do you know that we are goners too? If we stay out here, the Rees or the Bloods will get us for sure. This old man will die by the time we get out of his ear shot, so why not move on while we still have our hair?" Hugh was semi-conscious. He could hear his colleague's cruel logic and he feared its result. He could not speak, move, or gesture. Much of the time he was not even conscious, and he had difficulty even opening his eyes. Hugh listened in a haze while he heard Jim argue back.

"Mr. Fitzgerald, we are under orders from Major Henry. We are getting paid good money to wait and care for Glass until he leaves this world. I ain't goin back on my word."

The second day passed and then the third and yet Glass still hung onto life. He showed no signs of dying any time soon. Fitzgerald feared that if they did not move on soon, they might get caught in an early snow, lose the brigade's trail, or get killed by hostiles. Even Jim began to grow more uneasy about all the many things that could happen to them if they stayed on any longer.

Finally, Fitzgerald turned to pleading. "Boy if you will just move along with me now, I will give you my share of the bonus. I only want to save my own hair and my own life. What do you say, boy?"

Jim replied, "No sir! I can't leave Mr. Glass. It wouldn't be Christian and would be dishonest to Major Henry. We would never be hired in the mountains again. No sir, by God! No sir!"

In exasperation Fitzgerald declared, "Boy, I'm leavin come daylight. You can stay with that corpse if you want to, but I'm savin my own hair. I will just tell the Major that both of you went under and I had to flee in order to save myself. You can come on when Glass dies. If you make it out alive, you will be a hero."

Now Jim started to panic. He was inexperienced, a poor tracker, and not much of a hunter. He knew he would not be able to locate Henry's men or the fort by himself, and he probably would not even be able to kill enough food to live on. He was so shaken that he could not make up his mind.

In the meantime, Fitzgerald gathered up Hugh's knives, pistols, lead, gunpowder and Hugh's famous rifle, Betsy. He saw no reason to leave such valuable weapons for the natives and he could always sell them for hard, cold cash or barter them for other goods.

As he watched Fitzgerald, Jim began to relent. He made Hugh's bed as comfortable as possible and left a kettle of water next to the dying man. However, he left no food or knives because Hugh was so severely wounded that he could not eat anyway. Surely, he would die soon and then he wouldn't suffer anymore. Jim only hoped that wolves, bears or other carnivores would not feed on Hugh while he was still alive.

Hugh could not believe his ears as he heard his two comrades discuss his demise. He wondered, "Why can't they stay with me? Why not try to carry me further on a litter?" He wanted to cry out but nothing came from his torn throat. He wanted to wave his arms, but they would not move. Because of his stress and effort to communicate, he passed out again.

By the time Jim caught up with him, Fitzgerald was already making quick tracks to catch up to the brigade. Fitzgerald assured the young man. "We will just report that old Glass died and that we buried him proper. We only took his weapons so they wouldn't fall into the hands of any hostiles. No one will believe that we could take a man's weapons if he was not already dead."

Later, when Hugh awoke, he was not sure if he was in heaven or hell. He had lived a rough, sordid and violent life, and he had violated most of God's Commandments, but he had also given much back to society. Perhaps God would forgive him and show him some mercy. And if not, then burning in hell couldn't be worse than his current pain. His body throbbed, his fever ravaged him, and he was extremely thirsty. He had already swallowed all the water Bridger left him in the kettle.

Eventually air bubbles ceased emitting from his torn throat and from his gashed back, so he started to breathe a little easier. He tried to move his broken body closer to the bubbling spring in order to relieve his blistered face and parched lips. His strength returned just enough to allow him to place his hand and face into the cool water. This relieved the pain to some of his wounds and soothed his lacerated throat. Later the same day he was able to reach out and suck on some of the ripe berries that dangled over his head.

After three days of cool water and juicy berries, some strength returned to his tortured body. As his body grew stronger, his mind began to clear, and now he focused on the discussions of his deserting comrades. The more he remembered of his abandonment, the angrier he became. He stoked his desire for revenge, which strengthened his drive to survive.

At last Hugh became lucid enough to see that Fitzgerald and Bridger had not only taken his knives, his pistols, his strikes-a-light, his flint, his steel, his lead and his powder, but most dastardly, they had taken his Hawken rifle, Betsy. How could anyone leave a companion in the wilderness without a rifle or knife? Hugh became obsessed by the desire to catch up with his deserters. His anger helped him endure his pain and suffering.

By the fourth morning he awakened to see a large rattlesnake asleep near his pallet. As fat a snake as Hugh had ever seen, it appeared to have recently eaten. In the cool of the morning, the snake could not strike so Hugh was able to crush its head with a rock. He then reached into his torn breeches and found his straight razor. Thank God! It was the only implement his associates had not stolen from him.

He sliced the snake's meat as thin as possible so that he could suck on the flesh and try to chew the precious nourishment. Finally, he swallowed what was left of the juicy morsel. He even tried to pulverize some of the meat by hitting it between two rocks. When he gained more strength, he dried the remainder of the meat and gathered what berries he could reach. With his new food supply, he started to crawl down the trail left by his two deserters. Though he could only crawl a few yards at a time, he moved ever onward.

At the headwaters of the Grand River, Hugh could travel west no farther, so he left the trail and moved in a northeasterly direction back toward the Missouri. At this time he cared not about attacking bears or hostile natives.

At times he recognized edible roots that the Pawnee

had taught him were nutritious, and he used pointed rocks and sticks to dig them up. One day he came across a buffalo carcass that had already been cleaned by wild animals, but he found a few bones with marrow that he retrieved by smashing them with stones. He mixed the marrow with the few berries he had left.

By September his hunger pains were almost unbearable when a pack of wolves came toward him chasing a young, fat buffalo calf. They tore out the calf's leg tendons and dropped it to the ground. The wolves began eating the calf while it was still alive. Hugh watched until they had eaten almost half of the calf, then he raised his body to his knees and flailed with a large stick. He yelled with his torn vocal cords until the wolves were frightened enough to abandon their kill. Hugh ate as much as he could, devouring the liver first. He then cut the remaining meat into strips with his razor and again dried enough meat for his travel.

A few more warm days gained him enough strength to move ever-farther north and east. Most of his wounds were healing now, except for the deep lacerations on his back. With the assistance of a large walking stick, he was now able to drag himself along at the rate of several miles each day. His desire for revenge continued to motivate him, but his dream of recovering his rifle took priority.

CHAPTER 25

In early October Hugh Glass came across a temporary camp of natives. Although he held some trepidation, he overcame his fear and proceeded into the village. Through sign language, he learned they were friendly Dakota traveling to the burned Arikara villages to pillage more corn and vegetables. The unattended fields were still producing.

The Dakota allowed Hugh to travel with them to the Arikara lodges. The Dakota shared some of their meager supply of buffalo meat with Hugh and showed him how to harvest and parch the corn. He also ate baked squash and other edible vegetables.

With his strength improving daily, he moved downstream in search of any white assistance. When he happened into a friendly village of Sioux, they treated the deep wound in his back, which by this time had attracted maggots. Larvae were eating Hugh's decayed flesh, but they probably saved him from gangrene poisoning. Not only did the Sioux succor Hugh, but they also gave him an old horse to ride so that he could travel faster in his quest for help and assistance.

When he at last reached the French fur post of Fort Kiowa, it was already the middle of October. Hugh learned that General Ashley had left the post two weeks before on his way to St. Louis.

The factor, Joseph Brazeau, said, "*Monsieur*, I have a Mackinaw boat heading up to the Mandan to re-supply our other trading posts. Tilton's Post was built by James Kipp and William P. Tilton for the Columbia Fur Company. The Canadians also trade there under the Northwest Fur Company, which has been bought out by the Hudson Bay Company. The trading up here is fierce. The captain of our boat will be *Monsieur* Antoine Citoleux and he will have six *voyageurs* to row and sail his craft."

When Hugh boarded the craft, Captain Citoleux said, "Welcome aboard, *Monsieur*. My interpreter is *Monsieur* Toussaint Charbonneau. He has lived and traded among the Mandan and Hidatsa for many years."

Hugh knew of Charbonneau. "Mr. Charbonneau," Hugh said, "I believe we have a mutual friend, sir. I have become a comrade of Edward Rose, who is also a guide and interpreter. He has spoken well of you."

Charbonneau laughed aloud. "*Oui, Monsieur*. I know Five Scalps very well. I knew him before he is a famous chief of the Crow. I knew him before he was a famous chief of the Arikara. I also knew him before he guided the stupid Astorians to the Rocky Mountains.. He and I have had several business dealings together. How is my old *ami?*"

Glass replied, "Well, I sure hope he is doin better than I am. He left Ashley's party to guide Jed Smith and his brigade to the Crow last summer. If he is still with Smith, they may be on the Green River. If he ain't, he is probably in the lodge of some squaw in Absaroka. Har! Har!"

They both laughed at the thought of Rose choosing between being with Smith or staying among the Crow. Hugh told Charbonneau of his tale of being mauled by a grizzly and then how his companions left him for dead, even though they had been paid by Major Henry to stay and care for him. He told Charbonneau that he was looking for the two men who deserted him so he could kill them and recover his stolen rifle.

Charbonneau was appalled. "*Monsieur*, I am old and have seen many things in these mountains, but to be abandoned in the face of death is the greatest fear of man. I thank my God that I have never known such treachery."

Charbonneau added, "My friend, you should also know that the outlaw chief, Elk's Tongue, has moved his band of robbers to the old earth lodges of the Arikara, which is one mile below the Mandan. I do not wish to meet with this chief again and I recommend the same for you, *Monsieur*."

Hugh replied, "Thank you very much, friend. I was wounded by them damn Rees in a fight last summer.

I sure don't want to meet up with them again anytime soon."

Meanwhile, things at Fort Henry were not going well. Folks at the fort were constantly harassed by the Blackfeet, the Blood and the Piegan. Black Harris, John Fitzgerald and James Carson decided to quit the mountains under these conditions, and they paddled their skiff down the Yellowstone toward the Missouri. Major Henry was able to obtain forty-seven horses from the Crow and moved all of his supplies and men to the junction of the Little Bighorn and the Bighorn rivers. He left written messages on Fort Henry's buildings telling his men and any other trappers he passed where he had relocated. However, this information was unknown to Charbonneau and Glass.

When Citoleaux's Mackinaw reached the mouth of the Cannonball River, Glass and Charbonneau gave their excuses and put ashore. They informed Captain Citoleux that they preferred to walk ashore for a while, and that they would meet him further upstream.

They sneaked under the cover of darkness past the Arikara lodges to the Mandan villages. Charbonneau helped Hugh get new supplies and a horse and sent him westerly toward Fort Henry. This time Hugh Glass was equipped with a rifle, small axe, knife, flannel capote, leather leggings, moccasins, blanket and a small kettle.

Glass rode out of the Mandan village on the twentieth of November, just as the weather was getting cold and icy. He was still weak, and he had to be careful with his feet to guard against frostbite. Riding a horse contributed to cutting off the circulation to Hugh's legs. While he struggled overland he just barely missed Fitzgerald and his cowardly little crew, who were busy paddling their skiff south toward the Mandan villages.

Black Harris stopped his boat at Tilton's Post to get fresh supplies and a drink of good, mountain whiskey. Major Henry did not allow alcohol in his command.

Fitzgerald turned white when he learned that Glass had just left his boat and was alive and well. Fitzgerald listened in fear when he was told how Hugh was going to kill him for deserting him and taking his rifle.

Citoleaux grinned broadly when he informed Fitzgerald of the anger that Glass felt toward him. He also told the party how close they had come to being massacred by the Arikara along with all of the French Fur Company men. He asked Black Harris to inform Brazeau at Fort Kiowa that the Arikara were on the warpath and that he should be on his guard.

Even Black Harris now condemned Fitzgerald for what he had done to Glass. Carson did not know that Fitzgerald was actually paid to stay with Glass until he died, but instead had robbed him and abandoned him. Black Harris, however, was present when the brigade left Bridger and Fitzgerald to care for Glass. He was also present when Fitzgerald reported to Major Henry that Glass had died, and that he and Bridger had given Glass a Christian burial. Harris did not speak to Fitzgerald for the remainder of the trip to Fort Kiowa.

Fitzgerald tried to think of a way out of his predicament. He could never return to the mountains because Glass would kill him, and he could never gain employment in St. Louis again, because when the story spread, his name would become synonymous with 'treachery'.

Hugh continued his search for Major Henry as he rode through early snows. When he reached the junction of the Yellowstone and the Missouri, he built a raft of logs and paddled across to Fort Henry. Although the post was abandoned, he found notes telling him to go to the junction of the Horn Rivers and he set off on foot. It took him until the end of January to reach the new Fort Henry on the Little Horn River.

In the meantime, Ed Rose hunkered down at the mouth of Lodge Grass Creek with Chief Rotten Belly's River Crow. They held several good hunts and obtained a good supply of buffalo meat and winter robes. Ed was just getting settled in his new lodge when the chief's younger brother, Yellow Belly, rode into camp with his hunters.

"White trappers are building a trading post at the mouth of the Greasy Grass," said Yellow Belly. "They have fled to Absaroka for protection from the Blackfeet and the Assiniboine. Their chief is a tall man, with black hair and eyes like blue water. Shall we allow them to stay in our country without providing us with goods?"

Ed immediately recognized that Yellow Belly was describing Major Henry and his brigade, and this news meant that he had closed his post at the mouth of the

Yellowstone and had moved his operation to the mouth of the Little Bighorn.

Ed said, "My chief, this is the company of my friend, Major Henry. He is an honorable man and he will treat your people honestly and fairly. I will go to him and see if we can be of any assistance to him."

The chief nodded his consent and sent Yellow Belly back to the white men with Ed. They rode down the Little Bighorn until they came to its junction with the Bighorn, and sure enough, the trappers were cutting and laying logs to build a post similar to the one Henry had at the mouth of the Yellowstone.

When Ed saw Henry, he said, "Major Henry, what are you doin up here in Crow country? I thought your men were gonna winter on the Yellowstone."

Henry said, "Rose, it's good to see a friendly face in this hostile country. The Blackfeet and Assiniboine have stolen most of my horses and I have lost seven good men. If I can't get a decent harvest of furs this season, I am going to quit this business and go back to my lead mines. I have been trying to get rich in the trapping business for twenty years and it seems all I can do is lose more money. General Ashley and I are in serious debt and near bankruptcy." Since Ed had never owned more than his clothes, weapons and a few horses in his life, he could not imagine what bankruptcy meant. Ed changed the subject.

"I have vouched for you with Chief Rotten Belly," Ed said. "He will allow your men to trap his waters until you find better digs after the spring thaws come. I left

Smith on the Wind River with the Mountain Crow. He intends to cross over the Rockies to the Green River when the passes become clear. I told him about the low pass below the Wind River Mountains. You can cross there even when all the other mountain passes are still closed. The Crow use the southern pass to trade with the Shoshoni and the *Nez Perce*."

Henry's blue eyes twinkled as he asked, "Is there another pass below Union Pass? When I crossed over those mountains before, I used Togwotee Pass, and I damn near froze to death. Rose I am in dire need of some horses. Can you persuade the Crow to accommodate me?" He humbly added, "Rose, I want to thank you for the service you have always provided me and for your assistance to General Ashley. You have had many raw deals, but I can vouch for your honesty and reliability. If the General or I can ever be of assistance, just call upon us."

Ed was embarrassed, because very seldom did anyone thank him for his service. Only Colonel Leavenworth had praised him for his aid in negotiating and for serving as an Army Ensign during the Arikara War last year.

Ed looked Henry in the eyes and said, "Major I promise you as many horses as you need. By the way Major, we almost lost Smith comin across the Black Hills. He was attacked by Old Ephraim himself. Yes sir, that grey bear damn near killed him. It tore his ear off and chewed his scalp somethin awful. However, when I left him in the Wind River Valley, he was makin some improvement. He won't ever look pretty again, but he seemed as confident as ever."

Henry raised straight up as he exclaimed, "Good Lord! You have probably heard that I lost one of my men when we were coming up the Grand River. I think he was a friend of yours, old Hugh Glass? I paid two of my boys to stay with him until he died, and then they came in to Fort Henry and reported that they had buried him. They even had all of his weapons."

Ed was shocked, because he and Hugh had become good friends coming up the river, and they were comrades-in-arms during the Arikara War. They had both been pirates in New Orleans and both of them had lived for some time among various tribes. Hugh was the one mountain man Ed felt he could trust, especially if his life depended upon it.

Ed was sad when he departed with Yellow Belly to obtain some Crow horses for Major Henry. He rode in silence because he could just never talk to the stoic Yellow Belly. Although the man was a great warrior, he was a sour individual and spoke very little. And yet his brother, Chief Rotten Belly, was loved by all. Ed loved communicating with the chief.

Ed brought forty-seven horses back to Fort Henry, where he hung out with some of his old acquaintances. It was good to speak English again, and to joke with Americans, after spending so much time living among the Arikara and Crow.

At the onset of the new year, Major Henry promised

his men that he would open a couple of kegs of whiskey for the occasion. He did not drink himself and usually did not allow his trappers to drink, however, morale was low and he felt a little alcohol might just lift their spirits for the holidays. He had already experienced several deserters and he did not want to lose any more men.

Just as the men were getting into their second keg of good old mountain firewater, George Yount and Orange Clark came running into the fort. "Boys! You all won't believe your eyes! Get ready boys. You are not gonna believe it." Before anyone even had an idea what they were talking about, a thin, haggard, ugly, scarecrow of a trapper limped into the post. His white hair was ragged, and patches of it were missing, revealing horrible scars on his scalp. He carried his wolf skin cap in his gnarled hand.

No one seemed to know who the stranger was. Finally Yount yelled, "Don't you know him, boys? It's our old comrade who has risen from the dead. It's our messmate, Hugh Glass, himself. Boys, he is alive!" Ed was the first to grab and hug his old friend, even though he still could not recognize him. Hugh began to cry as he held on to Ed.

In the back of the room a trapper dropped to his knees and began to sob. "I'm sorry Mr. Glass," said Jim. "I'm terribly sorry sir. May God forgive me for I will never forgive myself. I didn't want to leave you, but Fitzgerald made me do it. I swear to God, he threatened to leave me if I didn't go with him and then he threatened to kill me if I told anyone that we left you alive."

Hugh's heart went out to the young man and he put his mangled hand on Bridger's head. He then offered in a squeaky voice, "James my boy, I heard everything you and Fitzgerald talked about while I was lyin there, but with my torn throat and injuries, I just couldn't communicate with you. I will swear to the Major and the men here that you wanted to keep your obligations, but that cowardly skunk Fitzgerald forced you to go with him. I forgive you boy, but just tell me where to locate my rifle. I have been stayin alive by my desire for revenge and to get 'Betsy' back. Where is my 'Hawken' boy, and where is the mangy coward that stole her?"

Major Henry stepped in, "Glass, I paid those boys to stay with you and to care for you. I'll fine this boy for leavin you, but you'll have to catch Fitzgerald on your own. He is out of my jurisdiction now because he, Carson and Black Harris have quit my employ and gone down river. I reckon you will find them at Fort Kiowa. I'll outfit you and give you a horse so you can cut across the prairie, and perhaps you can catch them at the fort. I'll also send three men with you to inform General Ashley that the route to the upper Missouri has been closed by hostiles. We will have to find an overland route to the Rockies by way of the Platte River drainage."

Ed shook Hugh's hand and said, "Glass, I have got to stay here with the Major, but I wish I was goin with you. However, I'm afraid they would hang me for killin a white man. I wish you good luck and I'll see you down the river in the fall. Keep your powder dry and I hope you find old 'Betsy'."

CHAPTER 26

Hugh and Major Henry's messengers cut across the prairie to the Powder River, and followed its western headwaters until they reached the Platte River. They then built a bullboat and began to paddle their way downstream toward civilization.

When they reached Pawnee territory they ran into the menacing Chief Elk's Tongue and some of his Arikara outlaws. Hugh did not know that he had just missed being killed at their village, which was just one mile below the Mandan villages.

Elk's Tongue tried to entice them to come ashore and he even pretended that he and his party were friendly Pawnee. Just as several of them stepped out on the bank, Hugh alarmed them, "Boys, I was raised by the Pawnee and these fellows ain't Pawnee. They are Rees for sure. I fought those devils just last summer, and that skunk in charge over there is old Elk's Tongue, the meanest Ree on the Missouri River. I say let's slowly back the hell out of here."

Dutton paddled his bullboat backward as fast as he could, which left the other men no choice, except to dive in and swim for their lives. Having been a pirate in New Orleans, Hugh was a good swimmer, and he swam into a beaver dam where he hid himself.

Hugh's companions were killed and the Arikara searched for Hugh Glass for hours without success. Hugh again lost his rifle and many of his supplies, but he still had his knife, his steel and his shotpouch. He waited until dark before he felt safe enough to leave the beaver lodge and head for Fort Kiowa. When he finally arrived, again ragged, hungry and torn by his struggles with nature, Hugh learned that Fitzgerald and Hugh's precious rifle had gone on down to Fort Atkinson.

By the time Hugh paddled into Fort Atkinson, he was again in a fit of anger and ready for revenge. He reported to Captain Bennett Riley, "Captain I am lookin for a skunk by the name of John Fitzgerald. The man robbed me and left me for dead on the Grand River and I'm told he is in your fort."

Captain Riley replied, "Mr. Glass, I have already heard of your story from a Mr. Black Harris. He stated that he was there with you when Fitzgerald volunteered to care for you, and that he was also present when Fitzgerald reported to Major Henry that you had died. I cannot allow you to kill a private in my Army, but I can return your rifle to you, because he still has it in his possession. He must have coveted your rifle very much indeed, to have held on to it after the hideous acts he committed against you. Wait here and I will retrieve your weapon."

After some time Captain Riley returned with Hugh's weapon and presented it to him. "Here is your rifle, sir," said the captain. "Please accept the Army's apology, and be assured that we will do everything in our power to see that Private Fitzgerald is well punished for his treachery." The captain continued. "Our Sixth Regiment has heard of your story, Mr. Glass, and they have raised three hundred dollars to compensate you for the transgressions against you. Please accept this money with our best wishes."

Hugh was overwhelmed with the generosity of the soldiers at the fort. The money would not pay for all his pain and suffering, however, if he could not kill Fitzgerald, at least the money would give him a new start in life. Therefore, he took the captain's donation and made plans to seek his fortune anew.

It was now June 30, 1824 and Hugh felt he had been through the ordeal of a lifetime, yet he had finally been reunited with his rifle, Betsy. Hugh said goodbye to Major Henry, Rose and his messmates before he took the next boat to St. Louis to invest his fortune.

When the weather cleared, Major Henry moved his men up to the Wind River Valley. Ed Rose led them to the mouth of the Popo Agie River, where the Major sent John Weber and thirty trappers over the headwaters of the Popo Agie to the Sweetwater River to locate South Pass. Ed drew lines in the sand to describe the pass that crosses from the Sweetwater River to Pacific Creek and on down the Sandy River to the Green River. The Crow and other Indian tribes called the Green by the name 'Seedskadee' or Prairie Hen River.

Henry then sent parties up the Little Wind River to its fork. They had some trapping success along the many creeks and rivulets, clear down to the river's junction with the Popo Agie. He sent another group up Sage Creek to all of its branches.

Ed led four trappers up the Little Popo Agie to its headwaters where they crossed over to the sources of *Beaver* Creek and descended to where it emptied into the Little Wind.

When summer ended, Henry pulled his men together and inventoried his harvest of fur. He said, "Boys, we have done pretty good this year, and I want to get back to St. Louis before we lose anymore men or peltries. Build us some bullboats and let's paddle down the Wind and Bighorn Rivers back to Fort Henry.

The men were feeling pretty high about their good catch of furs, and they were eager to get back to civilization to spend their wages. They had a rough time passing through Wind River Canyon, so they rested and repacked their boats at the Bighorn hot springs. Major Henry passed out a few gifts to each band of Crow they encountered while they descended the streams. Ed had told Henry to follow this procedure in order to build goodwill for future trips into Absaroka.

When the flotilla reached Fort Henry, the major was again devastated. A marauding war party had dug up some of their supply caches and then had burned Fort Henry. Ed checked out the ruins of the post and told Henry, "Major, the outlaws were Hidatsa, not Black-feet."

Henry told his men, "Boys, they have stolen my powder, lead, blankets, clothing, traps and kettles. Therefore, Fort Henry is no more."

They packed the few traps and supplies they could salvage and descended the Yellowstone. In route, Ed, who had been hunting along the shoreline, came running to the boats.

He alerted Henry, "Major, there are hostiles on the large island below Cedar Creek. I recommend we group our boats together and run the south side of the island. The river is just a little wider there and if we lay down a heavy barrage of fire they may back off and allow us through. They are the same Hidatsa that sacked Fort Henry and all of them are experienced warriors."

Henry brought all his boats in close and directed his men, "Boys, I don't want you to fire until I give the word." By now the trappers were experienced mountain men, and they were not going to be deterred by a few savages. Just when it looked like they might sneak past the island, the Hidatsa began a fusillade of fire.

Henry hesitated just a few seconds before he yelled, "Fire men! Fire! Fire at will!"

Their bullboats traveled at about eight miles per hour with the current, but it seemed an eternity before they cleared the blistering attack from the island. When Henry was able to pull ashore, count heads and tend to the wounded, he learned that they had lost four men outright and several men were wounded. They had been lucky, but they still had to pass the main Hidatsa and Mandan villages, so they buried their comrades and continued on their journey.

When they passed the main earthen lodges near the Knife River, the village seemed almost deserted. Ed made an observation, "I believe they are on their fall buffalo hunt, and we will not be hindered by those who are still left in their villages. I recommend we move on as quickly as we can."

Henry seemed to age and weaken with each new crisis. He resolved that no matter how well he and Ashley did this season, he wanted out. He was getting too old for this kind of life; besides he had been in the mountains for the past twenty-five years. He was ready to return to his lead mines and a calmer style of life.

Just when he felt the worst of the trip was over, a war party of Sioux began harassing them from the prairie shoreline. "They want us to pay them some tribute for allowing us to pass," said Ed. "They feel we are too cowardly and too beat up to defy them. Also, they feel like the white men are weak after observing us in our war with the Arikara. Many of these same Sioux men were there when the Rees made fools of us and they say that the Ree chief, Elk's Tongue, is still killing white trapping parties up and down the river."

Henry was flabbergasted. "By God," he yelled, "enough is enough! I will not give these heathen another damn farthing. Fire at will men! Shoot their damn heads off! I will die before I give in one more time."

The men rallied around their leader and began firing into the Sioux as fast as they could load and shoot. Some of the men were not even slowing down to tamp the ball into the barrel of their guns. They simply applied the powder, dropped in a ball and bounced the stock off anything solid to set the ball and then fired again. They were not very accurate in their haste, but they put up such a fierce line of fire that the Sioux soon retreated from the riverbanks.

Henry's boats quickly outdistanced the retreating hostiles and all firing ceased. The men gave a sigh of relief and even began to see some humor in their situation. They had no more encounters on the way to Fort Kiowa, where they replenished their supplies, their food, their powder and their lead.

Joseph Brazeau, the trader for the French Company at Fort Kiowa, greeted Henry. "*Monsieur,* he said. I lost six men to the Arikara chief, Elk's Tongue. The heathen has just about wiped out my trade on the river. I do not think I can return next season, no? Will you clear your debt this season, *Monsieur?*"

Major Henry bowed his head and sighed, "Just about Joe. I'm just about even I reckon. It's up to General Ashley if we return. I lost four of my men to the Hidatsa on the Yellowstone where they robbed me blind and burned Fort Henry. However, we couldn't find them at their villages when we came past the Knife and Heart rivers. Ed Rose says they were on their fall hunt. Oh, by the way, Hugh Glass and Toussaint Charbonneau made it through the Arikara, and Glass has left the mountains and returned to St. Louis. Old Charbonneau stayed among the Mandan."

Brazeau said, "Well, that seals the keg, *Monsieur.* If the Army does not assist us, we are finished on the river. We can no longer obtain credit when we are robbed and half-killed, no?"

Henry waived *adieu* to Brazeau and launched his new skiffs down river. He felt much safer now that he was rid of the awkward bullboats. When they reached Fort Atkinson, Ed Rose, Jim Beckwith and several other trappers left the expedition. They were looking for new jobs, and the prospects looked better at Ft. Atkinson than they did in St. Louis, because the competition there was fierce. Henry did not reach St. Louis until the end of August 1824.

CHAPTER 27

When Henry sold his furs, he found that they would barely clear the debt that he and Ashley had incurred for the campaign. His hopes for a fortune were dashed once again. He no longer had the drive necessary to lead the field supervision of the Rocky Mountain Fur Company.

"General," he said to Ashley, "I want to sell my interest in our venture. Do you think you can find a buyer?"

Ashley knew his friend was not putting his heart into the business. Henry no longer seemed aggressive enough to succeed in such a competitive field. Ashley had prepared for such an eventuality. "I am sorry to see you leave, Major," he replied. "However, I feel I can now turn field operations over to Jed Smith. We have some good boys out there, but he is the brightest and most farsighted. I will help finance his buyout."

Ashley purchased his new supplies and prepared to take them to Jed Smith in the mountains. He wanted to personally inform Jed that he was his new partner in the Rocky Mountain fur enterprise.

In the meantime, James Clyman half-walked, half-crawled into Fort Atkinson. He told this tale. "I got lost from Smith's party and I was down to my last eleven bullets. I thought if I turned back, I might not find Smith or I might find hostiles. I couldn't defend myself so I just kept goin and I killed just enough game to dry jerky and survive until I could get here."

Two days later Tom Fitzpatrick came into Fort Atkinson with conflicting news of the Rocky Mountain Fur business. He sent a communiqué' to Ashley, "General, we made a grand haul in furs and I was bringing them over South Pass and down the Sweetwater River when I hit a canyon between the mouth of the river and Goat Island and all my fur bales sank in the river. I was out of ammunition and near starvin, so I hurried on to Fort Atkinson with only a few of the furs that I could extract from the river."

He continued, "They are in a deep hole of water no one can locate except me. When I rest I will take some men and go after the remainder of our furs. I can sell the furs I brought with me to purchase horses and supplies so I can retrieve the cache on the Sweetwater."

Meanwhile, Ed checked around for Hugh Glass. He did not know where Hugh had gone or which trapping party Hugh had joined. However, Ed learned that Sylvestre Pratte had taken one hundred men on one expedition, that Ceran St. Vrain had left with a wagon caravan of trade goods, and that William Becknell had taken trappers on an expedition to trap the headwaters of the Gila River. Ed finally learned that Hugh had financed a trapping brigade and had left for Taos with Tom Smith, Jim Santiago Kirker, Ewing Young, James Ohio Pattie, Milton Sublette, Bill Williams, George C. Yount and Etienne Provost. In September Antoine Robidoux organized a trapping party and also left for Santa Fe. It seemed that the Mexican trade was becoming competitive with the Missouri trade. They were now trapping the Rocky Mountains from the south to the north.

Joshua Pilcher and the Missouri Fur Company were now in bankruptcy. Ed Rose felt it served Pilcher right after he had run roughshod over the natives, the army and every fur interest in the Missouri trade. He could not help feeling pleased at Pilcher's misfortune.

Ed Rose, Jim Beckwith and James Clyman joined Fitzpatrick in retrieving his sunken furs on the Sweetwater River. Ed convinced Fitzpatrick to purchase mules instead of horses for the expedition. Ed believed that the natives would be less apt to steal mules, and that mules would be more dependable and could carry heavier loads than horses. He also believed that mules could survive on less water than horses.

Ed knew that there were various other reasons the men should use mules instead of horses. He had learned that when a mule hit the trail, it would not drink until the end of the day. He also knew that a mule would eat almost any vegetation it came in contact with, which made them much easier to feed.

CHAPTER 28

When the party left Council Bluffs, the group headed southerly across the Platte down to the Big Blue and over to the Little Blue. They had hoped to locate the Pawnee for game but they were off on a buffalo hunt and their villages were abandoned. They continued in a westerly direction until they again came to the Platte. They followed the south bank of the river onto the prairie where it became much cooler and the grass drier. After they passed Cottonwood Canyon and Box Elder Canyon, timber became more scarce.

The first point of interest that caught Ed's attention was Sioux Lookout. From its perch he could see the entire countryside. Tom Fitzpatrick guided them continually along the south side of the stream until they came to the fork of the South Platte and the North Platte. Prior to the fork they crossed the stream and continued down the north side of the westerly stream. They ascended past several large rock monuments that would later become trail markers for those seeking South Pass.

Ed thought, "If I could write, I would make maps for folks who wanted to cross the country. I could even become a guide and lead them."

As it was he would just have to commit everything to memory as he had always done. One formation he saw was a cylindrical tower rising from the top of a conical hill. He guessed the entire formation to be about three hundred feet high and it could be seen for miles. Next they came to an area of bluffs, which were also on the south side of the North Platte. When the party reached the mouth of the Laramie River, Ed saw how clear the stream was and judged it to be about one hundred feet wide.

When they passed the Medicine Bow Mountains they came to a valley about ten miles wide with numerous antelope, buffalo, mountain sheep and good grass. The streams that bordered the valley were covered in small willows and stocked with beaver. Northwest of the Medicine Bow range they slowed to only five to six miles per day and the snow ranged from three to five feet deep. About the only fuel they could find consisted of sagebrush and buffalo dung.

Ed kept an eye out for Sioux hunting parties who were now claiming hunting territory along the North Platte and the headwaters of the Powder River. They followed the bend of the river in a southwesterly direction until they approached the mouth of the Sweetwater River. When they came to a canyon where the stream was restricted to a deep whirlpool, Fitzpatrick set up camp.

"Rose," said Fitzpatrick, "you go up yonder and set up a lookout. Keep a sharp eye out for any renegades what might want to rob us of our furs and mules. Beckwith, you and Clyman strip off your britches and give me a hand divin for our furs. We've got to dive down to retrieve the pelts and this water is so cold that they will be as fresh as the day they were skinned. Now, get to it boys."

Ed rode off, feeling thankful for his assignment. He located an outcropping with a good view and set up a dry camp. He sure would like a fire but he was experienced enough to know that the Sioux could see smoke for miles on the prairie.

Near the end of the day he heard two rifle shots in quick succession, which was the signal for him to return to camp. When he rode into camp he could not believe all the bales of furs they had brought out of the river. However, the men were almost frozen before they could pack all of the furs on the mules. Ed thought, "Maybe Major Henry sold his interest in the Rocky Mountain Fur Company too quickly. Perhaps General Ashley will have a productive year after all."

The trip back to Fort Atkinson was both joyous and uneventful. Ed talked with Beckwith as they rode. "Boy," he began, "how are you doin as a free trapper with these fellows?"

Jim replied, "Mr. Rose, I barely make enough to buy my traps, horses and supplies for the next season. I can't ever get any credit ahead on the company books. They pay me poorly and charge me double for my supplies and necessaries."

Ed laughed, "Boy, that's why I joined up with the Crow and the Ree. If I need a new gun, I just trap some beaver or I trade with some buck who will take my goods down to some fur post. I always have some credit at Ft. Kiowa or some other post. When I need horses, I just join in an Indian raid and steal some new ones from some other tribe. And women, Boy, I have all the women I ever need. They love white men, especially dark ones. Waugh!" Ed continued, "When I hear of some expedition comin up the river, I just hire on as a guide or interpreter. Why don't you try to join up with the Crow yourself?"

Jim laughed loudly, "I sure would like to find me some friendly women. I need somebody to wait on me and care for my lodge and my personal needs. I can't afford to hire women like some of the 'booshways' do."

Ed added, "Old Greenwood has just taken himself a Crow wife. He wants to winter-up with them and learn the Crow language. I can help you get lined-up with them because I'm still a chief in good standin in Absaroka."

Ed wintered at Fort Atkinson while he waited for any trading party traveling on the river. As luck would have it, General Henry Atkinson and Indian Agent Benjamin O'Fallon were planning just such a venture.

The U. S. Government and the U. S. Army were concerned about the number of Americans who had been killed in the mountains in recent years. Also, the British were gaining the advantage in mountain and river trade with the Indians. The Northwest Company joined the Hudson Bay Company and built Fort Vancouver on the

Columbia as well as buying Fort Astor from John Jacob Astor, which they renamed Fort George. David Thompson built Kootenae House on the upper Columbia River. Now, the British controlled the Red River of the North, the Milk River and they were making inroads into trade on the Missouri River.

O'Fallon and Atkinson were made co-commissioners to lead a peace treaty expedition up the Missouri and Yellowstone to pacify, and to some degree, to intimidate the Native Americans. No one in the United States was more qualified to serve as their guide and interpreter than Edward Rose. Based on the recommendation of Colonel Henry Leavenworth, General Atkinson hired Rose to be their interpreter.

In his letter of recommendation, Colonel Leavenworth wrote,

> "...Rose was a brave enterprising man, well acquainted with the Indians. He had resided among them for about three years. He understood their language, customs and they were much attached to him."

> "...the Arikara called to Rose to take care of himself before they fired on General Ashley's party. This is all I know of the man. I have since heard that he was not of good character but everything he told us was fully corroborated. He was perfectly willing to go into their villages and did go in several times."

Colonel Leavenworth, General Atkinson, General

Ashley and Major Henry were all satisfied with the services of Edward Rose. Ed was excited about his new assignment, but he dreaded working with O'Fallon, especially after the story that Hugh Glass had told him about the temperamental Indian Agent.

The Treaty Commission not only included O'Fallon and Atkinson as co-chairmen but assigned Angus Langham as the secretary and John Gale as the surgeon for the expedition.

General Atkinson began at once to redesign the numerous keelboats that would be needed for the expedition. He ordered the boats fitted with wheel mechanisms to relieve much of the drudgery of polling, pulling, rowing and cordelling the boats upstream.

The men would power the boats by pulling and pushing crossbars connected by pitman gears to the side-mounted paddle wheels. The wheels were twenty feet in diameter and were attached to a vertical shaft that was attached below a cogwheel about eight feet in diameter. These wheels were inclined twelve degrees and had a motion of three and a half revolutions per minute. They revolved on a horizontal shaft that was cogged and to which a waterwheel is attached. The waterwheel turned twenty times per minute, which gave the boat a velocity sufficient enough to travel up the Missouri River at the rate of two to three miles per hour.

With a crew of good boatmen, General Atkinson expected to make twenty-five miles per day, which was twice the rate for normal keelboat travel, and the method would prevent a great deal of fatigue upon the men.

However, later in their journey, Atkinson abandoned the treadmill system due to the many breakdowns and instead, he made the men sit on benches along the sides of the boat and then push horizontal slides in unison, which went through a gear mechanism, then turned the paddlewheels. The first boats properly equipped were christened *Beaver, Mink, Muskrat,* and *Raccoon.*

On September 17, 1824 Major Stephen Watts Kearny assigned his men to the boats. In total, Kearny had ten officers and one hundred fifty-six non-commissioned officers, musicians and privates of the First Infantry. Additionally, he also had some civilians under his command. Desertion became common in this expedition from the beginning. One soldier committed suicide, one died of natural causes, and one died from an accident.

The *Mink* was to be the command boat for General Henry Atkinson and his staff. In the meantime, the *Otter* was being rigged with the paddle wheel apparatus in St. Louis and it finally departed up the Missouri in October 1824. However, the boat became iced in near the mouth of the Kansas River, and it did not reach Fort Atkinson until late in the spring.

The *Lafayette* belonged to the Fort Sutler. He used the boat to carry goods to restock the various traders' stores on the upper Missouri. However, he loaned his boat to the expedition to carry additional supplies. Each soldier required a minimum daily ration of twelve ounces of bacon, twelve ounces of hard bread, four ounces of whiskey and four ounces of beans. Food and whiskey alone totaled sixty-two tons. The boat also carried five tons of clothing, arms and ammunition, with three tons of gifts for the Indians that they would treat with. Cannons, stores, tents and spare parts amounted to over seventy tons.

Finally on May 16, 1825, all eight-wheel boats sailed forth from Fort Atkinson to ascend the Missouri River on the 'Yellowstone Expedition'. Some of the cavalry were mounted, and the men rode until the flotilla reached the Great Bend of the Missouri. Here the horses were to be returned to Fort Atkinson.

At dawn each day the men boarded and traveled on their assigned boats until midmorning. They stopped for one hour in order to have breakfast. They then boarded again and sailed until early afternoon, when they would stop for a one-hour dinner break. The third part of each day found the boats sailing along until twilight, when the men docked and made camp for the evening. Only an occasional mechanical breakdown caused a break in the daily routine. When Ed and the commissioners met with the various tribes, treaty-signing ceremonies usually lasted several days. In all, twelve treaties were signed.

Ed kept busy riding out to locate the various nations and trying to bring in representatives to sit at the treaty table. He also served as an interpreter for the commission during treaty negotiations. The only military man he could relate to was a young army lieutenant named Reuben Holmes.

Lieutenant Holmes usually escorted Ed in search of the tribes. Holmes also was responsible for ordnance for the expedition. He became infatuated with the dark, heavily scarred interpreter.

"Mr. Rose," Holmes asked, "how did you come to the mountains?"

Ed looked off across the prairies and shielded his eyes as he looked for telltale sign of a native camp. Slowly, he turned to the lieutenant and answered, "I reckon I came because the Good Lord and the Devil fought for my soul and the Good Lord just barely won out. He has sent me to help the Indians get along with the whites and to help the whites learn to respect the Indians. They call the Indians 'heathens' and they are not at all. I've never seen anyone more religious than the Indians. They pray to about everything and they even carry special rocks to pray to. They pray to the sky, the water, the sun, the moon, the trees, the grass, the buffalo, the earth and anything else that they fancy."

Ed continued, "I went to the mountains with old Manuel Lisa and Major Andrew Henry. I was so impressed with the Crow that I've been with them most of my life since. They are like the family I never had. My ma was Cherokee and Negro, but my pa was a white trader. He never showed me any concern except to sell me to apprenticeship at a warehouse on the Ohio River in Louisville. I worked for the wharf-master loading boats."

Again he stared across the horizon. "He was good to me only because I was strong and a good worker. I was doin all right until a damned French boatman showed up drunk and started beatin me. I went loco and we went after each other with our knives. He cut my nose damn near off and slashed my cheek here as you can see. I didn't know anything about knife-fightin, so I beat him to death with my fists."

Holmes looked at Ed's tortured face and asked, "How did you get away with murder? What kept them from hanging you?"

Ed slowly smiled for the first time. "The wharf-master was a good friend and he was like my real father. I was badly wounded and he stowed me on the keelboat of a friend who shipped me to New Orleans. By the time I arrived I was almost well, but I was missin most of my nose. I took up with a Cajun boatman that took me down to Barataria to get well. It was there that my friend and I got into the pirate trade for a few years. I learned to shoot, trap, steal and fight for my life. I rebelled when the Lafite brothers tried to press me into service on their pirate ships. I fled upriver to St. Louis and here I am."

Lieutenant Holmes was fascinated with Ed's tales and his experiences. He had never met anyone like Ed before, not even in the Army. As the Yellowstone Expedition ascended the Missouri, Ed and Lieutenant Holmes grew closer. As the lieutenant learned more about his guide and interpreter, he began taking notes and keeping a diary.

Several years later, in 1829, Lieutenant Holmes published his notes regarding Ed Rose in the St. Louis Beacon newspaper.

CHAPTER 29

After each treaty signing, General Atkinson put his troops on a full dress military parade; they fired their rifles and a six-pound cannon. They loaded the rifles with fireballs and signal rockets to impress the natives.

Although Ed cautioned Atkinson about trying to pick his own leaders for the Indians, the general persisted in selecting chiefs and sub-chiefs. Atkinson gave the leaders medallions embossed with a likeness of President John Quincy Adams. At the conclusion of each ceremony, the commissioners distributed presents, guns, powder, lead, chief's coats, knives, blankets, tobacco and whiskey. To keep up this tradition, the commission had to purchase an additional three tons in gifts from the American Fur Company.

As the flotilla ascended the river, men continued to desert the group. Most were caught within a day or two, hungry and in tattered clothing. Some men deserted several times and eventually were never heard from again.

Hunters went out often to seek fresh game to supplement the military's meager diet of pork, flour and hardtack. Just below the Kansas River, the flotilla reached the old site of Fort Osage. In 1808, George Sibley had originally built the post as Fort Clark; it had been built to protect a government-owned trading 'factory'. Sibley was later appointed the 'head trader' or 'factor'. He had recently married Mary Easton and was now being appointed to survey the Santa Fe trading trail for the government.

The post was erected on a bluff, which commanded a beautiful view of the river. It was a pentagon-shaped stockade sporting log pickets perforated with loopholes. Two blockhouses were situated on opposite corners, with a small bastion on one side. Inside the perimeter, two buildings served as quarters and storehouses.

On the fifth of June, Ed hailed Stephen Watts Kearny. "Captain, I have been sent by Captain Armstrong to get more supplies. We have been with the Ponca's for over a week now and we haven't had any game."

Kearny turned to his sergeant. "Draw Rose enough pork, bread and rations for a week." To Ed, Kearny said, "Tell Captain Armstrong that we will join him within two days and that we will bring medals and gifts for the chiefs."

Early on the eighteenth of June, General Atkinson ordered the guard to mount in full dress and parade with the military band. The General wanted to impress the tribes as Ed brought them in to council. Ed and Black

Harris brought in a band of Cheyenne who had treated with Atkinson and O'Fallon near the mouth of the Teton River.

Finally on June nineteenth, General Atkinson reported to O'Fallon. "Major, the river rose over two feet last night and it is still swelling. I have a report that the *Raccoon* has broken her crank. She was detained at the White River yesterday, but she should join us some time today." Captain Gantt finally brought the *Raccoon* in at dusk and they camped about a half a mile below the main camp and on the opposite shore. The boat broke its crank again and could not join the other boats.

Ninety Yanktons and Yanktonas also came to the opposite side of the river during the night. Meanwhile, the *Mink* and the *Beaver* proceeded upriver and joined the flotilla above the Teton River.

The Ogallala were only six miles up the river and the Saone thirty miles, while Ed had to bring the Cheyenne eighty miles. He assisted Captain Armstrong and Lieutenant Waters in escorting all the tribes to council with the commissioners.

On the thirtieth of June, Captain Kearny addressed Ed. "Rose," he said, "we need some fresh meat for our larders. Can you scout along the Teton and try to locate a buffalo herd?"

Ed rode up the stream with Lieutenant Waters and some of his mounted soldiers until they came to a small valley that Ed had seen before. He covered himself with bushes and crawled along the ground as the mounted men observed from a hillock. They watched as Ed moved very slowly, trying to look like a bush, staying downwind of the small herd. He knew that buffalo can smell exceedingly well but they had poor vision. Ed fired his rifle; the men saw the puff of smoke before they heard the report of the rifle. The herd milled around some, but seemed confused because they could not see their attacker. Ed kept repeating the same process until he was able to shoot six buffalo before they stampeded out of the valley. The military men were astounded at Rose's feat.

Ed rode back to the lieutenant. "Yo! Lieutenant Waters," he hailed. "You can go ahead now and direct your men to go down there and butcher the six buffalo that I downed. I had to let some of them get away so they could raise some more calves. Like the Indians, we need to leave some food for another day." When the men brought in the meat they found it weighed over three thousand pounds; it fed the troops for over four days.

On the second of July, Ed brought Chief Standing Buffalo and two hundred fifty Ogallala warriors to treat with Atkinson and O'Fallon. The head chief was very dignified, well behaved and had great influence among his people. They set up over one hundred lodges while the military troops caught a large number of fish for a big feast.

On the fourth of July, the Ogallala held a dog feast ceremony for the commissioners. The Cheyenne and Saone seated themselves on buffalo robes and beaver skins so they could also partake in the feast. All attendees joined in passing the peace pipe. On the fifth of July the Army provided a parade review for the Indians.

Lieutenant Holmes arranged for their large cannon to be mounted on wheels and drawn by horses at full speed across the prairie near the ceremony. The display impressed the natives enormously, but they were in total awe in the evening when the lieutenant set off twenty rockets. The native people could not understand how the shells could be fired from the gun but would not explode until the shells made impact with a target. Their rifles could not do such a thing.

The next day, treaties were signed by the Ogallala, Cheyenne and Saone. All the chiefs were given horses, holsters, pistols and swords. Chief High-back Wolf of the Cheyenne gave General Atkinson a mule and a saddle.

Again, Lieutenant Holmes fired six more shells with his Howitzer and the resulting explosions made lasting impressions on everyone present. When the boats departed, over three thousand natives lined the shore to see the peace commission ascend the river.

Ed rode off again, this time in search of more buffalo and Chief Fireheart's Sioux tribe. It was not until the fourteenth of July that he arrived in the new village of the Arikara. Chief Elk's Tongue had leased the village of earth lodges from the Mandan and had promised to not attack other tribes or white men on the river. The Arikara did not live up to any agreements they made and often raided any party that showed they had anything of value.

There were now twenty-five hundred Arikara in the village. The resident trader and interpreter for the tribe was Joseph Garreau. He and Ed had been friends for many years, but Garreau had become a drunk. Since the war of 1823 he had been bitter with Americans because Joshua Pilcher had burned all his trade goods.

When Captain Kearny brought up the boats, Ed set up a treaty meeting for General Atkinson with the Hunkpappa tribe. Their head chief was Little White Bear. Atkinson gave him medals and gifts before they retired to the Arikara village for a feast in the General's honor.

When Ed set up the meeting he had hoped to interpret for the Arikara, but instead they had selected old Garreau as interpreter. Ed no longer trusted Garreau and watched the man closely. Problems arose almost at once when O'Fallon began to rail against the Arikara regarding their raids upon Missouri Fur Company posts and other posts on the Missouri. Chief Bloody Hand of the Arikara became defensive and arrogant.

O'Fallon barked, "You have been raiding Missouri Fur Company fur posts and attacking white men on the upper river. Your people killed four Rocky Mountain Fur Company employees on the Platte River last year. The army will punish any future transgressions by your tribe."

The commission punished the Arikara by only giving them a modest four hundred plugs of tobacco. The only medal they gave was to Chief Bloody Hand, a serious man with a Roman nose, round face and harsh eyes. The corners of his mouth formed a permanent scowl. Designs painted on his war shirt depicted his many exploits and achievements. In exchange, the Chief offered the General seven horses, a pile of buffalo meat, and a large number of earthen pots.

After several days of high winds and rain, the hunters located a herd of elk and buffalo for fresh meat. Because of the rains, mosquitoes overwhelmed the military troops. Bloated buffalo carcasses started flowing down the flooded river. Wolf packs followed and ate the carcasses that caught on river snags.

On the twenty-second of July, the hunters brought in seven more buffalo, an elk and eight deer. Ed was able to locate a herd of over two hundred buffalo opposite the Cannonball River.

By July twenty-seventh the flotilla arrived at the Mandan villages on the Knife River. O'Fallon dispensed tobacco and the Mandan put on a dance exhibition. The Mandan and the Hidatsa were neighbors, allied through their cultures and through intermarriage. They consisted of five villages of over two hundred earth lodges that were located between the Heart and Knife rivers.

Chief Wolf of the Mandan was austere and respected, yet overbearing and feared. He was the son of the famous Chief Le Bourne, or One Eye. The second chief was Mah-to-tah-pa or Four Bears and the shaman was Old Bear. The top of Old Bear's face was painted red, while the bottom half was painted black. Four Bears had a strong face, equine nose and sunken cheeks, but he was a generous gentleman, elegant, brave and handsome. The Hidatsa chief was Two Crows, a man with a protruding chin, equine nose and slanted eyes.

Kenneth McKenzie operated the trading post among the Mandan. His interpreter was Toussaint

Charbonneau. By now, Charbonneau had lived among the Mandan and Hidatsa for almost thirty years. Ed had known him since 1808 and he had traded and traveled with Charbonneau. At one time they had even purchased Arapaho maidens from the Shoshoni and then sold them to trappers in the Powder and Yellowstone valleys.

The American Fur Company supplied McKenzie's trade goods for the Mandan. The peace commission stayed among the Mandan waiting for flooding to subside. While they waited, several of the officers followed the Mandan onto the prairie to see a buffalo surround. The hunters killed over fifty animals and provided a big feast for the military.

That night a violent storm blew down the tents and drenched everyone in the villages. However, on the thirtieth of July the commission finally signed treaties with the Hidatsa and Mandan. The commissioners gave them many presents and medals.

Ed was able to bring the Crow in for a treaty council on the third of August. The Crow party consisted of three thousand civilians and six hundred warriors. All of them rode their finest horses and wore fine beadwork. Atkinson again ordered Lieutenant Holmes to set up the artillery. After they gave the tribe a running display of the cannon, Holmes had his men line up review.

The commission set up the peace tables for the Crow. However, during the conference, O'Fallon learned that the Crow held a Blackfoot woman and child captive. He told Ed to demand their release.

"My chiefs," Ed interpreted, "I want the immediate

release of your prisoners. I have my entire army and our big guns here to back my demand."

Rotten Belly responded to Ed, "Tell the white blowhard that the Sparrowhawk people have adopted the Pecuni woman and child and we will not give up our family." During the heated discussion that followed, O'Fallon suddenly rose and slammed his pistol against Rotten Belly's head, laying his skull wide open and causing blood to run down the chief's face. O'Fallon then quickly hit Chief Red Bear and Chief Two Crows. He was even trying to shoot Chief Long Hair before Ed grabbed Major O'Fallon by the arm and took the weapon away from him. General Atkinson arrived just as Ed put a stop to the assault.

The General demanded, "My God Major. What have you done? What is happening here?"

O'Fallon cursed. "These damn Crow have two prisoners and refuse to turn them over to me. I had everything under control until Rose stepped in and stopped me."

Ed turned to Atkinson. "General, when Crow warriors capture women and children, they adopt them. The captives become Crow and a part of their extended family. If they give them up after that, they are givin away their family. Besides, Sir, they have spiked your cannons and the cannons couldn't fire now if you wanted them to. If a fight starts, those guns will blow up and then they'd wipe us out for sure."

Atkinson turned to O'Fallon. "Major, let us sign our treaty and give them plenty of presents. We don't want a war with the Crow. They are one of the best allies we have in these mountains and our fur companies need them. Let's just make our apologies and get on with the signing our treaties."

O'Fallon cooled and grudgingly abided by Atkinson's wishes, but he would not forgive Ed for embarrassing him before the natives. He would not be outmaneuvered by a bunch of heathens and a nigger. At the same time, Ed knew he would have to be careful from here on out and stay clear of Major O'Fallon. The man was as dangerous as Hugh had figured him to be.

Charbonneau and one of his wives boarded the *White Bear* when it sailed from Mandan to try to catch up with the flotilla. A war party of Assiniboine followed the boat to the mouth of the Little Missouri River. Charbonneau watched nervously as he kept an eye out for his friend, Ed Rose. He knew Rose had fought against the Assiniboine several times and that Ed did not consider them competent warriors; nevertheless, Charbonneau feared all tribes.

The marauding hunting parties caused game on the prairies to become very scarce. Even though there were numerous swans on Goose Egg Lake, no one wanted to venture forth to hunt them with so many enemy warriors loose in the area.

It was ironic that the boat camped below Charbonneau Creek, which was named after Toussaint by William Clark himself. Clark gave the creek that name after Charbonneau guided Lewis and Clark on their journey to the Pacific Ocean in 1805.

On the twelfth of August Ed and Black Harris

brought in six elk and four deer for the commission larder, and on the thirteenth they killed three large grizzlies near the Burnt Hills. As they passed the mouth of the Yellowstone, Ed pointed out Fort Henry to the commissioners while Black Harris brought in four deer and a white bear from the area.

Atkinson made an observation. "Although I have been opposed to building a new fort on the Missouri, this location could be the most beautiful position to defend on the river. It can also be a self-sufficient operation because the area abounds in buffalo, elk, bighorn, deer, antelope, ducks, pigeons and fish. It is indeed the key to the Rockies." Little did Atkinson know that he was looking at the future site of the most successful trading post on the Missouri River, 'Fort Union'.

They observed a large herd of buffalo in the bottom between the two rivers and Ed decided to ride out to scout the herd. While he was gone, General Atkinson decided to unload all boats and thoroughly clean them before reloading and repacking everything. He had done this several times before while they were ascending the river. Lieutenant Holmes set up a blacksmith shop and a forge to repair the broken machinery. Atkinson sent the *Elk* and *Raccoon* on up the Missouri while he worked on the *Beaver, Muskrat* and *Mink*.

Ed rode past Fort Henry and saw that one entire wall had been burned. There were holes dug up all around the post where marauding tribes had been looking for caches of furs and goods left by the white traders. He continued riding in a southwesterly direction as he ascended the Yellowstone. When he neared Fourmile Creek, he glimpsed another rider in the willows. He quickly hid himself in the brush and eased forward for a better view. He dismounted and cocked his rifle as he peered through a small tree.

Suddenly, a black face with a large rifle was looking right back at him. Both parties yelled at the same time, "White man! White man!"

When they recognized each other they roared with laughter. Ed yelled first, "Damn you, Beckwith. You ain't no white man."

Jim laughed. "Hell Rose," he said, "how can anyone as black and ugly as you call himself white? You are too damned scarred up to be white and you are darker than I am."

They walked together for an hour, leading their horses and laughing before they mounted again. Ed said, "I'm guidin the Atkinson-O'Fallon Peace Expedition. We are getting ready to go on up to the falls before we start back down river."

Jim said, "I'm with General Ashley – we have a pot load of furs. We could sure use a hand gettin the furs back to St. Louis. I can't remember how many bullboats we have sunk."

Ed said, "I'll go find General Atkinson and tell him Ashley is comin down the Yellowstone. I'll make sure he waits at the mouth of the Yellowstone until your boys can get down there."

With that Jim rode off toward the Bighorn River to locate Ashley's party while Ed rode on back toward the

Missouri. On Friday, the nineteenth of August, General William Ashley's brigade of one hundred twenty-five men brought in one hundred packs of prime beaver fur. The *Buffalo* and *Otter* loaded Ashley's furs and all of his men before they began to descend the river.

In the meantime, Atkinson sent the *Mink, Beaver, Muskrat, Elk* and *Raccoon* on up the Missouri toward Great Falls. The main body now consisted of three hundred thirty men and one cannon.

By the twenty-ninth of August the boats had descended to Charbonneau Creek again. Hunters brought in twelve elk, including three by Captain Armstrong, one by General Atkinson, one by Lieutenant Harris and one by Lieutenant Vanswarengen.

On the first of September the *Mink* broke a 'pitman' on the wheel boat mechanism. While it was being repaired, about five o'clock in the morning, a large buffalo bull raced into camp. It knocked down all the tents, tables and mess that had been set up for the commission. The bull finally jumped into the river before being shot by Major Kearny. The big bull was happily added to the meager larder of the crew. On the fourth of September an iron hoop on the rudder of the *Muskrat* broke. The party landed at the Mandan villages to repair the hoop on their trader's blacksmith forge.

By September the seventh, the flotilla again arrived at the Arikara village. Six chiefs from the Saone clan of Sioux came aboard General Atkinson's boat and received five guns, two pistols, blankets, scarlet coats, powder, lead and other gifts.

The expedition passed the Grand Bend of the Missouri and arrived at Fort Kiowa on the ninth of September and they passed Cedar Island on the eleventh of September. Ed took the commission to the Ponca and issued tobacco, five blankets, four coats and various other articles to their chiefs.

The next day he took them to the Maha and the Yankton Sioux. Two kegs of whiskey were issued to them against Ed's recommendation. The *Muskrat* hit an underwater snag in shallow water and the *Otter* and the *Beaver* came to their rescue. They were able to raise the *Muskrat,* bail out the water and drag it onto a sandbar. They repaired it during the night and were able to save all supplies, including the beaver, the ammo and their officers' baggage.

On September the fourteenth and fifteenth, hunters were able to kill five black bears and seven elk. The flotilla at last returned to Fort Atkinson on the nineteenth of September. They had been gone for over four months and they had traveled over two thousand and seven hundred miles. Ashley had shipped one hundred packs of fur weighing nine thousand seven hundred pounds worth a total price of forty-eight thousand dollars.

Major Henry had sold out too soon.

CHAPTER 30

As the flotilla descended the Missouri, on October 12, 1825, the group stopped for dinner at the trading house of Francis Chouteau. Francis had recently married and his new wife served as hostess. While the commissioners dined, Ed went to look for the Kansa and Kickapoo tribes, traveling through high winds and light snow.

The flotilla was still suffering from desertions. Ed and the other hunters went out daily to find game to feed the military operation. A few days after they stopped, they found a great deal of game just above the Grand River.

In the meantime, General Ashley was finally able to pay off his debts. He obtained financing from the American Fur Company to outfit his expedition into the Rocky Mountains next year. He obtained $20,000 to outfit sixty men and a hundred sixty horses and mules, with enough merchandise for his rendezvous in Cache Valley. The general was busy. He was engaged to marry

Miss Eliza Christy on October 25, 1825. Eliza was the daughter of an established, prosperous and well-known resident William Christy, who arrived in St. Louis in 1810 and quickly became the second largest landowner in the city. In addition, Christy was now the Registrar of the United States Land Office. As a wedding present, Christy gave Ashley a ninety-eight thousand square foot city lot so that the General could build a new home.

On October 31, Jedediah Smith left St. Louis and traveled west on the Kansas River, northeast along the Republican Fork, before getting bogged down with the winter snows. His party lost one third of their mules by early January 1826, and he decided to set up his winter camp among the Pawnee.

Smith called Jim Beckwith and Black Harris into his lodge. "Fellows," he began, "I need to send you both back to St. Louis to request that Ashley purchase extra horses and send a relief expedition to bring us aid. If we don't get reinforcements we won't be able to get to the Rockies by the spring hunt. I'm depending on you both."

Harris was already an experienced mountain man but Jim was still learning his craft. Harris directed Jim, "We've got to pack as much as we can carry because we have to walk to St. Louis. First, we have to get some raw-hide and willow branches to make us some snowshoes. We'll need to carry some extra hide strips and branches for repair because these shoes will wear out after while." Jim was young, strong and willing take on any new experience, but he was not eager to walk in snow all the way to St. Louis. It took several weeks of trudging rough terrain and cold weather to finally reach the city and locate General Ashley.

Harris said, "General, I have been sent by Mr. Smith to get some more men and mules. He said you would know what else he needs. We have lost about a third of our pack animals and several of our men have already deserted. Captain Smith and the men are bedded down with the Pawnee to wait for your help."

General Ashley answered. "I reckon you boys are tuckered out, so go over to Le Barrra's Hotel and charge the bill to me. I'll give each of you twenty-five dollars in silver now, and I'll keep the rest of your accounts on my company's books for a future draw. I will also give each of you chits so you can eat or drink at any of the local cafes or saloons. I have already recruited some men, including Ed Rose, who both of you already know. You can find Rose down on the waterfront. I'll let you boys know when I'm ready to travel."

Ashley recruited a total of twenty-five men, including Rose, William Sublette, Jim Beckwith and Black Harris. The expedition left on the eighteenth of March 1826, and traveled along the north shore of the Missouri. The terminus of the Santa Fe Trail was now located in Franklin. That's where Ashley purchased horses and mules. After getting fully equipped and mounted, Ashley's party proceeded on up the Missouri River to Fort Atkinson.

The Rocky Mountain Fur Company relief party left

the river at Fort Atkinson and moved westerly along the Platte River to Grand Island. They finally located Smith's brigade among the Pawnee on April 1, 1826.

Ashley immediately addressed Smith. "Jed, you and Harris go on to the Green River so you can arrange a new rendezvous in Cache Valley on the Bear River. Tell any trappers you meet along the way that my supplies will arrive there in June."

General Ashley appointed Robert Campbell to the position of field general and the caravan continued westerly along the North Platte. Ashley maintained a rigid military system of discipline and organization, and the party made good time with minimal problems.

The group ascended the Sweetwater River to South Pass and then rode over the continental divide to Dry Sandy, Little Sandy and Big Sandy, and then traveled on down to the Green River. When they descended the Green to Ham's Fork they met seventy-five trappers who had been alerted earlier by Smith and Harris that they were coming. Ashley traded with them for two days, then moved his supplies across the front range of the Uinta Mountains to the Bear River and on down to Cache Valley.

When Ashley's men arrived at the rendezvous on May 25th, they were met by a brigade of Iroquois trappers who wanted to trade furs for new supplies. They were soon joined by Smith, who had made peace with the Shoshonis and had brought some of them to the rendezvous.

Eventually a hundred trappers, with their native

wives and children, joined in the trading activities at the rendezvous. Everyone joined together in songs, dancing, shouting, trading, running, horse racing, jumping, telling yarns, target-shooting, frolics and every other extravagance that could be invented by mountain men and natives alike. Festivities became wilder as more of the whiskey barrels were uncorked.

Ashley collected one hundred twenty-five packs of beaver, which would be worth over $60,000 back in St. Louis. He paid his free trappers three dollars a pound for beaver at the rendezvous. For those trappers who elected to work for the company and draw a basic salary, he paid only two dollars a pound. They were paid a base salary whether they obtained any beaver or not.

Although Ashley hoped to get five dollars a pound for his furs, he had to pay $1.12½ per pound in order to deliver the furs to St. Louis. Therefore, he stood to profit only about eighty to ninety cents per pound.

On the fourth of July, everyone fired their weapons and the alcohol flowed freely as a good time was had by all. The natives did not understand the celebration, but they needed no explanation in order to enjoy the festivities.

Once the rendezvous was over, General Ashley conferred with Jed Smith, Bill Sublette and David Jackson to discuss the future of the Rocky Mountain Fur Company. Ashley knew he could possibly make a small fortune this season from his furs, and if he combined that with the harvest he made in 1825, he could pay off his debts again and earn a sizable profit. He did not want to jeopardize his gains with any possible future losses because the competition was increasing.

Ashley called his brigade leaders. "Boys," he said, "I took Smith in as a junior partner this year and he has done very well for himself. I'd like to sell my interest in the Rocky Mountain Fur Company to you fellows, and I can still provide you with supplies and merchandise each summer for three more years. All of you know the system works and you boys will do just fine as long as you can find new beaver streams."

Smith asked, "General, what will my part in the new company consist of?"

Ashley answered, "Jed you have been a good man to take over for Major Henry, and I am going to credit you with $5,000 for your share in our present partnership. I have about $16,000 worth of merchandise remaining and I will transfer the contracts of forty-two of my trappers and their catches for 1827 into the company."

He continued, "Jackson, you and Sublette can put up $3,200 in furs to meet your requirements for a piece of the partnership. That leaves an indebtedness of $7,800 due in beaver in 1827. I will contract to supply by July 1, 1827 for between $8,000 and $15,000 worth of new merchandise at specified prices. I will meet your trappers at the south end of Bear Lake. I will also agree to not sell to any other individual or company while I am under contract to you."

After all parties agreed to the conditions of the sale, Ashley left to return to St. Louis with fifty men and a hundred horses and mules laden with pelts. Ashley set a record by reaching St. Louis in only seventy days and then received a record $80,000 for his furs.

When Ed learned that his old trapping partners were successful and that General Ashley had become rich, he decided that he too needed a slice of this good fortune. He had always wanted to be important and influential among the mountain trappers and the natives. He could only remain a free trapper if he stayed tied to the Rocky Mountain Fur Company, but he thought he needed a new approach. He decided to seek employment with their competitor, the American Fur Company out of Fort Pierre. Because AFC was expanding up the Missouri, they would need experienced interpreters and traders.

Ed pulled Beckwith aside. "Son, I have a way that you and me can get some of this wealth. Why should just the white people get rich? Come with me to the Crow and I can make us both wealthy and powerful."

Jim answered, "I have been doin real good as a free trapper. I have money on the company books and I get to lead my own brigade from time to time. Besides, I don't speak Crow. Old Greenwood never did have time to learn me any. I was lodged with him and his wife last winter and I didn't learn nothin."

"If you move in among the Crow," Ed explained, "some pretty gal will teach you Crow real fast. Just come on along to the Crow when you are ready to make somethin of yourself."

Jim Beckwith returned to trapping as a free, but

poor, trapper on the Snake River. Meanwhile, Ed Rose slowly rode back to the Mountain Crow on the Bighorn River with very little to show for his many efforts during the past two years, except some new thoughts for his future.

CHAPTER 31

Jim Beckwith was having a rough time as a free trapper. He opened a small trading post among the Blackfeet and married the daughter of Chief Heavy Shield. He did pretty well until he killed his wife in a fit of jealous rage. Only the chief's interference saved Jim's life. The Blackfeet took Jim six miles from the camp and turned him loose, telling him to run for his life. And run Jim did. He ran all the way back to Cache Valley to rejoin his comrades.

On January 6, 1829, Jim signed a promissory note with William Sublette of the Rocky Mountain Fur Company for two hundred seventy-five dollars. The note was payable in beaver at the July rendezvous at the rate of three dollars for each pound of fur.

Jim discovered that General Ashley charged trappers different prices and even doubled the prices for the men from the Hudson Bay Company. He paid some free trappers five dollars a pound for their beaver while he paid Canadian deserters only two dollars per pound. The

As these trappers then purchased their supplies, they were shocked by the mountain prices. Coffee and sugar were one and a half dollars per pound each. Tobacco was three dollars per pound, gunpowder two dollars a pound, fish hooks were one and a half dollars per dozen, scissors were two dollars each, flints were a dollar, knives cost two and a half dollars, blue cloth was five dollars per yard, lead was one dollar a pound, blankets were nine dollars each, and buttons were one and a half dollars per dozen.

Jim was disgusted. He owed more than he usually made and he could not get ahead. He was also having personal problems with many of the other trappers. His bragging, practical jokes and tall tales annoyed many of his comrades.

Jim departed with William Sublette and James Bridger to trap on streams feeding the Snake River. While camped on Henry's Fork, friendly Shoshoni told them that an outlaw band of Punak Shoshoni were camped about three miles below them.

Sublette told the kindly Shoshoni chief, "Tell them that if they harm one of my men or steal one item from my camp, I will hunt them down and wipe them out."

Meanwhile, Jim had become friends with a Shoshoni brave named Singing Bird. This Shoshoni brave came to Jim and Black Harris to ask for help. "Brothers, will you go with me to the Punacks? My relative, Badger's Tail, has taken my finest buffalo chaser and will not re-

244

turn him. Since the Punacks are not honorable, I need your assistance."

Jim and Harris were both interested. They wanted to inspect the Punak camp to look for a few horses and mules missing from the Rocky Mountain Fur Company herd. The trio strode up the stream on foot. When they approached the Punak camp, Singing Bird called out to his relative, "Badger Tail, I wish the return of my spotted buffalo chaser."

His scruffy relative yelled back, "You owe me a horse. I took a horse. Now we are even."

Singing Bird was so angry he hollered, "You no longer have relatives. In the eyes of our family, you live no more. Your name will never again be called." These were very angry words to the Shoshoni. To be without relatives was to be as good as dead, to be of no account.

Badger Tail drew an arrow from his quiver and fired it into the chest of Singing Bird, doubling him over in pain. And just as quickly he pulled his large knife and charged, cutting Singing Bird deeply in several places, mortally wounding him. Black Harris and Jim fired their rifles at Badger Tail, dropping him to the ground. Then they immediately turned and ran for their lives.

As they neared their own camp, they yelled for assistance. Sublette and Bridger roused their men and came running to meet Jim and Harris. They fired into the pursuing Punak warriors, sending them back into the woods.

As soon as he could breathe, Jim spat, "Them bastards have killed poor Singing Bird. They stole his best horse and now they have killed him."

Harris added, "There's about five hundred of those Punaks and they're armed to their chins."

Sublette turned to Bridger. "Gabe, take two hundred men and teach them a lesson they won't soon forget. Now get goin.'"

To white men and Shoshoni alike, Bridger yelled, "Let's go boys. Grab your weapons and follow me."

Jim jumped upon his horse, raised his Hawken and rode off upstream toward the Punak village. When the party reached the village, it was vacant. Everything was in disarray; the camp had been vacated in great haste. They followed the trail of the Punaks fleeing across the foothills and down to the Green River. There they spotted the Punaks on an island in the middle of the river.

Bridger said, "Beckwith, you take some of the boys and ride across the stream and flank them. I'll take the rest and ride abreast of them on my side of the river. We'll catch them in a crossfire, then by God, we'll have 'em for sure."

When they were abreast of the island, all parties opened fire. Since logs and rocks were limited, the Punaks could not build a fortification to protect themselves. The trappers and their superior rifles cut the enemy down. In a few minutes it was over. The only human beings left alive on the island were eight women. Bridger took the women back to his camp and turned them over to the Shoshoni in payment for the life of Singing Bird. The Shoshoni followed the age-old tradition that day and adopted the captive women into their tribe.

The party had taken over four hundred scalps that day. The Shoshoni held a great scalp-dancing ceremony. While they were celebrating and dancing, Ed Rose and a large party of Crow rode into camp.

Greenwood told the Crow quite a story. "Beckwith," he began, "was a Crow, and when he was a babe he was captured by the Cheyenne. He is now a great trapper and a great hunter among us white men. Beckwith killed and scalped many of those Punaks by himself and he has the scalps to prove it."

Ed almost laughed at Greenwood's tall tale but the Crow could not wait to return to the Bighorn to re-tell the stories they heard from the Shoshone and Caleb Greenwood.

Jim said nothing to dispel Greenwood's story about Jim's heritage. He even felt honored with the acclaim given him by the Crow. Ed Rose just nodded and said nothing to his native friends to disprove the story. He would just be still and see how far the Crow would go with this story about Jim. If all went well, this could be Jim's invitation to go live with the Crow.

For the fall hunt Jim went with James Bridger, Robert Campbell and thirty-one other men to the Powder River, where Jim planted six of his traps before returning to camp. While sitting around the camp, Jim offered, "I reckon I'll just catch me more beaver this day than anyone here. I figure I'll get me a plew in every trap I set."

A French-Canadian, Pierre LaBat, groused, "*Monsieur* Beckweeth, you do everything, no? You catch the pink elephant, no? I think *Monsieur* is the big wind from the North."

Jim chuckled, "I'll be here when you're gone, Frenchie. I was weaned on beaver and I know how to catch them for sure."

Jim left early the next morning to run his trap line. When he set out his traps, he used a twelve-foot float pole that was four inches in diameter. Because of the pole size, he had never lost a trap. Yet, when he came to his last trap, it was gone. Jim looked everywhere for that trap to no avail. Soon he began to suspect Labat of stealing his trap. Since he could not accuse the Canadian without some evidence, he called upon his friend, Jim Bridger.

Beckwith asked, "How bout it Gabe, can you help me look for that lost trap? They're damned expensive and besides, I need to know if I'm bein humbugged."

They went up the stream again and Jim showed him about where he had anchored the trap. Bridger scoured the ground in the area and then pointed, "I see sign where the trap came out of the creek and dragged itself up this trail. Follow me."

They slowly tracked the dragging trap up a trail, away from the stream, and over a dry creek bottom for over a mile. Suddenly they saw something in the brush attempting to drag the trap chain, which was making a great racket. Jim stepped forward and fired his rifle to stop what he thought was a badger or a beaver.

When they investigated the deep brush, they found a beaver dead in Jim's trap with the chain still attached. At the end of the chain was Jim's twelve-foot float pole.

Bridger began to laugh. "See this curly hair in the chain? A buffalo must have caught his head under the trap chain and it hung up on his hump. He then dragged that squallin beaver, chain, float pole and all, to this spot before he could dislodge it."

The party laughed all the way back to camp. Jim could hardly wait to get to the fireside to tell the tale of what had happened to his beaver trap. That night when he finished his story of the lost trap, LaBat grunted, "*Monsieur*, this is the worst lie yet, no? You exceed yourself this time, I theenk."

Jim rose to his feet, "This time Frenchie, I've got me an eye witness and it's old Gabe there. He's the one that discovered that a buffalo had stolen my trap. Har! Har!"

The big French Canadian was embarrassed; he had lost face in front of his comrades. He smacked Jim hard along the side of his head. Before he knew what was happening, Jim drew his Green River knife and then the Frenchman grabbed his own. The trappers around the fire acted quickly and pulled the two apart.

Bridger took Jim away from the camp for a few days of trapping to allow things to cool off. When they reached a fork in the stream, Jim took one branch while Bridger took the other.

While Jim plodded along he thought about his life and his current situation. He was still dissatisfied. As he came into some thick willows, he detected a horse herd secreted in a small patch of thick buffalo grass. Before he could determine to whom the horses belonged, guards suddenly surrounded him. Jim had wandered into a large Crow hunting party. He quickly raised his rifle overhead with his left hand and pulled his knife from its scabbard and held it up into the air with his right hand. The Crow took his weapons from him and led him along the creek bank.

Jim looked across to the other fork of the stream, and saw Jim Bridger in the distance. He thought to himself, surely old Gabe would see him and report to their brigade that Beckwith had been taken captive by the Crow. If Gabe reported quickly to Sublette, a rescue party could come to his aid before he and the Crow left the area.

While the Crow were departing from the area, Jim remembered the tale that Greenwood had fostered upon the Crow about Jim actually being Crow and about his Crow relatives. With this in mind, Jim began to pretend he was actually the Crow that Greenwood had described. He signed to the party that he wanted to see his relatives. He also signed that he too was a Sparrowhawk. The confused warriors took Jim with them to their camp on the Bighorn River.

In the meantime, Bridger reported to Sublette, "Old Beckwith has gone under this time for sure. He couldn't even put up a fight. They just up and grabbed him before my eyes. They have killed him sure enough. He wasn't a bad sort of a fellow. We've done lost us a good trapper."

CHAPTER 32

The Crow hunting party rode into the village amid great excitement. Not only did their braves have many new horses for their clan but they had a captive as well. The captive was a black man, like their own famous warrior, Five Scalps. Everyone began to mill around and inspect Jim.

He was allowed to dismount from his horse and he looked around for some one in authority. His eyes focused upon a female who was tall, attractive and who carried several war weapons. He thought it strange that they allow a woman to carry weapons of combat. Perhaps she was the female warrior that Ed Rose had told him about. Although she was dressed as a young woman, she did fit the description Rose had given him.

Jim began to sign to anyone who would pay attention to him that he too was a Sparrowhawk. Rose had advised him to never use the disparaging word, 'Crow'. He was also told to never call a girl or a woman a 'squaw'.

These words were considered disrespectful and degrading to the Sparrowhawk people.

Several young men pushed forward. They had been in the Shoshoni camp when Greenwood told his tale of Jim having been stolen by the Cheyenne when he was a boy. Several older people also remembered such a raid by the Cheyenne and some had lost children during the attack.

Women began to file by and examine Jim from the top of his head to his feet. They almost undressed him in their zeal to locate their lost child. Finally, Antelope Heart, the wife of Big Bowl, identified Jim as her own son because of a mole near his left eyelid. She began to cry and hug Jim until they were actually lying upon the ground.

To Jim's surprise, he was even attacked by four of his new sisters. They were all hugging and crying, while more family members appeared. Jim was afraid he had overdone his lies this time. He realized that this story had the potential of exploding in his face if someone appeared who could show him to be a fraud.

In the meantime, he was not only alive but he was the most popular brave in Absaroka. He lost track of the tall, young woman he had seen upon his arrival in the village, but he would inquire about her later. His new family dragged him to their lodge and began to feed him. They placed him in a high bed of honor in the back of their lodge.

He was handsomely redressed in the finest garments Big Bowl could provide and his smelly mountain clothes were quickly discarded. Jim slept for a long time because he was worn out by the entire ordeal. For several days new friends and relatives visited him. Each of them brought food and several gave him horses. He noticed that one or two of the animals had even been stolen from Bridger and Sublette, but of course, he didn't say anything about that.

His sisters began teaching him some of the Sparrowhawk language; they also began looking for potential wives for him. No great warrior his age should remain unmarried.

Jim inquired about his mentor, Five Scalps. He let anyone he could communicate with know that Five Scalps was his dear friend and would help him get established as a trader among the Sparrowhawk people. He had not heard from Rose since his arrival and he was anxious to get some advice from him. He worried about his charade and about being exposed.

When the season changed, Jim was courting the three daughters of Black Lodge, a well-known warrior. They were Three Roads, Still Water and Black Fish. After a short courtship, Jim selected Still Water as his wife. Black Lodge consented and directed that a wedding feast be prepared in his daughter's honor.

According to Crow custom, from the day they married, Jim was never to speak to his father-in-law or mother-in-law again. His new brothers gave him a fine horse herd as a wedding present. Not only were his rifle and Green River knife returned to him, but he was given a beautiful bow, a fine quiver filled with straight arrows, a lance, a shield and a decorated war club. He was now a fully equipped Crow warrior.

Jim's new wife made him content in his new life and the chief gave him the new name, Morning Star, to honor him as the lost son of Big Bowl. Jim began to trap the local streams, hunt in the canyons and the hills, and learn the language and culture of his new tribe.

Joe Meek and Robert "Doc" Newell were greenhorns who were making their way to the mountains for the first time. They were employed by William Sublette as muleteers. They were responsible for packing and transporting over one hundred fifty thousand dollars in goods to the mountains for the men who made their living trapping beaver and trading pelts. The trappers would trade their beaver pelts for supplies and whiskey.

The caravan had followed the newly surveyed Santa Fe Trail as far as Bent's Fort before turning north along the front range of the Rockies and then they headed for the Platte River. They ascended it to the mouth of the Sweetwater River then cut across the bottom of the Wind River Mountains to the Popo Agie, which in the language of the Crow meant 'Head River'.

As the long caravan snaked its way down the river, Joe saw Sublette raise his rifle to halt the two long lines of pack mules. Joe and Doc Newell looked through the haze but saw nothing. Word came down the line, "Smoke seen. There's smoke down there."

Again Joe and Doc looked in vain. Finally, in the early afternoon, they saw columns of smoke coming from saw-tooth patterned lodges with a background of red sandstone, surrounded by dark shapes like buffalo. It appeared to be a good campsite with a clear mountain stream, belly deep grass and plenty of timber for fuel and building of forts and structures.

As they drew closer, the 'buffalo' became horses and mules grazing around the camp. They had been on the trail for over three months and man and animal alike began to increase their pace until the entire party broke into a headlong race to try to get to the camp first. They began to use the bloodcurdling yells of "Waugh!" and they fired their guns repeatedly. The date was July 1, 1829. The caravan had finally arrived. They had made the 'Rendezvous'. The party did not stop until they came to the large buffalo lodge that was the headquarters of the Rocky Mountain Fur Company. Joe, Doc and others began to unpack the heavily laden mules while Sublette opened a trunk and held mail call for all the trappers who had letters or newspapers from the United States.

Old friends were hugging, greeting, yelling, and talking, all at the same time. There were mountain men with their wives and children as well as native warriors with their families. Joe Meek quickly learned how a large camp operated. The head of a brigade or a large trapping party was called a booshway from the French word, *bourgeois*. Usually the clerk of the party was called 'the little booshway'.

The clerk carried all company's valuable papers and documents in two trunks, which were balanced on opposite sides of a mule packsaddle. The hobbled animals were turned out to graze under the vigilant eyes of horse guards.

Trappers were assigned to messes and had to provide their own cooking, which was usually done by camp-keepers. During trapping season the duties of the trapper was simply to bring in the beaver and leave them for the camp-keepers to skin and pack the furs into bundles. The same condition held for the hunters. They brought in the game and left it for the camp-keepers to skin, cut up or dry for consumption. The meat was then distributed to the various messes.

During inspections of the camp or firearms, anyone who failed inspection was fined in beaver skins. Someone else was then assigned to correct the deficiency and they were paid in beaver skins for their effort. If there was no beaver, the penalty and payment were recorded on the company books by the company clerk.

When Joe and Doc finished unpacking their mules they reported to Bill Sublette, "Captain," Joe enjoined, "What mess might I be with?"

Sublette answered, "You'll be with Jim Bridger over yonder. You best do a good job because you are replacin Jim Beckwith, who was a damn good trapper and was killed by the Crow last season. Newell, you will also be in Gabe's mess. By the way, the Indians call Bridger 'The Blanket Chief'. I advise you not to ask why they call him by such a name."

The new men gathered their gear and piled it up with Bridger's mess before they joined in the wild party known as 'Rendezvous'. When trade finally began, trappers and natives alike purchased foofooraw for their favorite women. Many trappers could barely get out of debt before they had to borrow against the next season's furs.

When alcohol started to flow, games of chance, along with contests and fights, spread throughout the camp. There were horse races, shooting matches, wrestling matches, footraces, and the telling of tall tales. In the latter, the mountain man excelled over all others.

CHAPTER 33

Zenas Leonard led his trapping brigade from the Great Salt Lake to the Green River and ascended to that stream's headwaters where they planned to make camp for the winter. Before they could even get their tents erected, they were visited by seventy to eighty natives. One of Leonard's men had once lived among the Crow and recognized their dialect at once.

Hall said, "Mr. Leonard, they say they're going after the Shoshoni and they saw our camp and came to check us out. They claim to be friendly. When I lived among the Crow, they were always friendly with white people."

Zenas replied, "Tell them they're welcome but we don't have any whiskey or food for them."

After Hall conversed with the Crow, he informed Leonard, "They say to thank you but they don't drink crazy water anyway and they have plenty of pemmican and jerky with them. They say they are from the River Crow on the Big Horn River." That night Zenas and his men became very complacent and did not even post guards for their horses. They hobbled them loosely so they could graze and chew the bark off the young cottonwood saplings.

When the first men arose for breakfast and calls of nature, a cry rang out, "The horses! The horses! We've been robbed!"

Zenas quickly determined that five of their best hunting horses had been stolen. The tracks led away from their camp and all the signs seemed to indicate that their Crow visitors were the thieves who stole their stock. They mounted the horses they had left and followed the Crow party over the Three Forks of the Missouri and down to the Bighorn River on the Yellowstone. They ascended the Bighorn until they found a Crow village at the mouth of the Stinking River.

They rode into the village and approached a Negro-looking man. The man hailed, "Halloo there fellows, where are you all bound for?"

Zenas was surprised to see a black man among the Crow and even more surprised to hear someone speak English. He responded, "How come you are livin among the Crow?"

The black man with the heavily scarred face smiled and offered, "I am York. I came to this country with Lewis and Clark. They took me to the Pacific Ocean with them back around 1805. I came back to this country to trade and to trap with Mr. Kenneth Mackenzie. The Crow treated me like a white man and since I wasn't treated that way before, in the States any way, I just naturally took to this country. So I settled down to stay. The Crow have made me a war chief and they listen to my advice."

Ed Rose was almost delirious with his tall tale.

Zenas was educated and was not taken in by the black man's ruse. True, he had heard of York, who was the slave of William Clark, and he knew that Clark had given York his freedom, but he had heard that York had moved into the Ohio countryside.

Instead of accusing the man of lying he offered, "Some Crow visited us a few days back while we were camped on the Green River and stole five of our best horses. We tracked them to this village. Have you seen them?"

"I've got your horses, boys," laughed Ed. "When the braves came into camp with those horses I knowed the animals belonged to some rich white men so I took them away from the young braves. I have the horses in my own lodge for their protection. If any chief protects a person or that person's property in his own lodge, it is as safe as it can be anywhere."

"When the Crow saw you in the Shoshoni country they thought you were tradin guns and powder to the Shoshoni. They simply took your horses in retaliation. If you all will just give me some trinkets or blankets, then I can get those boys to forget this entire incident and you can keep your horses."

Zenas knew that he was being blackmailed, but it seemed to be the only way to keep the peace. Perhaps they could also get some aid from these people. Zenas said, "We have a few trade goods, and if it will keep these heathens from stealing us blind, I'll provide them with a few trinkets."

Ed again smiled broadly, "You can stay among us as our special guests until the weather breaks. Since I'm a chief, I'll personally protect you."

When the weather cleared, Ed and the Crow decamped and descended the Bighorn to its mouth. Leonard took his men back to the Shoshoni.

The new year of 1832 was cold indeed. Many things were unfolding on the upper Missouri under the financing of the American Fur Company and John Jacob Astor. Kenneth Mackenzie built Fort Union at the mouth of the Yellowstone and James Kipp built Fort Piegan at the mouth of the Marias River.

Jim Beckwith and Samuel Tulloch built Fort Cass at the mouth of the Big Horn River. It was three miles below the river's mouth on the east bank of the Yellowstone. It was constructed of cottonwood pickets with bastions at the extreme corners. Jim said, "Tulloch, I sure would like it if you would hire Ed Rose to hunt and work for you here at Fort Cass. He has more experience than anyone on the river, but he is getting too old to trap and trade by himself. He sure helped me get settled with the Crow."

Sam replied, "Sure enough, Beckwith. I have heard of Rose's exploits ever since I came to the mountains. I know he was controversial at one time, but at his age, he isn't much danger to anyone. I can always use a good hunter and I can let him stay here in the fort as my interpreter."

Ed Rose didn't know that his protégé had obtained employment for him, but he was relieved to not have to live on his own any longer. His abilities were diminishing more each year. His vision was getting poor and his reflexes were slowing down. He was elated when Tulloch also hired his friend, Hugh Glass, who was even older than Ed. Together again, they enjoyed the cold nights around the fort fireplace where they could recall their experiences and try to out-lie each other.

In the meantime the American Fur Company had become the dominant company on the upper Missouri River. Paddlewheel steamboats were now being used to take supplies, trappers and guests to most of the fur posts and then return the furs to St. Louis.

Tulloch said, "Rose, I want you, Glass and Menard to take some traps and set them on some of the streams down river. We have not trapped the area for some time and I sure would like to get a few more bales of fur before the river thaws. You boys can pull your gear on the ice with a sled faster than you could pack it on horses. I will send you some new supplies in a few days."

Ed said, "We'll take care of it boss. I am anxious to get out into the country anyway because I'm getting lodge-fever just sittin around here."

Glass chided in, "Sure enough. The exercise might loosen my joints and bones. We'll let Louis here do the heavy pullin. Har! Har!"

The air was bright, clear and cold as the threesome began their assignment. The river was frozen solid and had a light dusting of snow, which made the sled glide easily down the ice. They were still in sight of the fort when a party of warriors on the opposite riverbank started shooting at them.

Glass asked, "Rose, can you make them out? Who are they?"

Ed said, "Boys, it looks like old Garreau and his outlaw band of Rees. If it is, we are in for a rough time because those Ree have never forgiven me for my part in the Arikara War. I think we best set up our defense right here because we can't make it back to the fort." They quickly built a wall around themselves with their sled and gear. Menard was frightened, but he joined in with his comrades when they returned the Rees' fire.

Ed urged, "Hugh, we will try to hold them off if you can make it back to Fort Cass and get us some help. Hurry as fast as you can." Hugh left the safety of their improvised fort and tried to run up the river as he sought cover along the riverbank. He only traveled a quarter of a mile though before the Arikara overtook him, killing and scalping him.

When Ed heard the commotion raised by Glass's capture, he realized the seriousness of their situation. "Louis," he said, "Hugh is a goner and we ain't gonna make it either. How do you want to die? Do we want to be taken alive and let those skunks torture us or do we want to go out with a bang and take as many of them with us as we can?"

Louis Menard's manner was now calm and deliberate because he had become resigned. "*Monsieur*, we have lived long and hard, and we have had a good life. We will fight until our death, no?"

Ed grinned. "Exactly like I figured it, Menard, old friend. We will make them pay dearly."

Rose and Menard fired their last shots at the Arikara and then began to strike out furiously with their knives. In a few moments, Ed lost consciousness as he and Menard were slashed to pieces and then scalped. Ed Rose had lost his first and last knife fight.

Garreau believed that the Arikara had finally achieved revenge by killing their old nemesis, Edward Rose. With a heavy heart, he gathered what remained of his Rees warriors and fled down river before Fort Cass could retaliate.

Edward Rose, 'The Five Scalps', was no more.

EPILOGUE

One of the guests at Fort Union was Maximilian, Prince of Wied. Maximilian wrote, "Glass, with two companions, had gone from Ft. Cass to hunt beavers on the Yellowstone and as they were crossing the river on the ice farther down, they were all three shot, scalped and plundered by a war party of thirty Arikara, who were concealed on the opposite bank."

John F. A. Sanford wrote to William Clark, "Glass, Rose and a man named Menard have been killed and scalped by the Arikara."

Jim Beckwith recorded, "... I, Pine Leaf, Yellow Belly and two hundred of my River Crow went to Fort Cass to trade. We set up our camp outside the fort and put our horses out to graze. The next morning many of them were missing, and when I went to look for them, I saw bodies lying on the frozen stream. I sent men from the fort to investigate and they found the bodies of three of our comrades."

They found Hugh Glass closer to the fort. It appeared that he was trying to get aid for his companions. They found Ed Rose and Louis Menard scalped and hacked to death on the icy Yellowstone. They had been shot before being mutilated. Rose was identified by what was left of his grey, curly hair and his many facial scars. Glass had not been disfigured.

In the words of Harold W. Felton, "Ed Rose helped his nation move forward. He was one of the first to face the western wilderness, and one of the best. What he did made it better and easier for those who followed and who will follow."

According to Hiram Chittenden, "... Rose was buried on the banks of the Missouri nearly opposite the mouth of the Milk River. On any of the old steamboat itineraries of the Missouri River may be seen among the names in that vicinity, 'Rose's Grave'."

Storyteller that he was, Jim Beckwith claimed many of Ed Rose's exploits for himself. Others made a legend of Ed Rose, or changed historical events to suit their own minds. In any event, the accomplishments of Ed Rose will live on in the history of the West, and fact or legend will hold Rose as one of the truly great contributors to our Nation's progress and success.

In any event, long live Edward Rose, 'The Five Scalps'.

THE END

GLOSSARY

A'caraho	In Crow the word means the Mountain Crow or "where the many lodges are."
A-ra-poo-ash	Chief Rotten Belly of the River Crow.
Absaroka	The Crow called their home Absaroka and were sometimes called the Absaroke or Absaruke people. They referred to themselves as the Sparrow Hawk people. The French word and the English translation erred by interpreting their name as "Crow."
Alcaldes	This name is Spanish for the mayor or civilian head of a Spanish or Mexican mission district in the New World. Sacagawea's son, Jean Baptiste Charbonneau, served as a guide for the Mormon Battalion in 1846-47 and was appointed the Alcalde of San Luis Rey Mission in Oceanside, California in 1847.

Algonquin	The language of the Arapaho, Blackfoot, Cheyenne, Atsina, and Plains Cree.
American Fur Company	The fur-trading company created by John Jacob Astor; the most powerful fur company in the United States.
Astorians	Wilson Price Hunt led an American Fur Company overland expedition to the Pacific Coast in 1811-12 to establish trade with the Far East. The trading post was named Astoria and the members of the expedition were called the "Astorians." The project failed due mainly to the War of 1812 with the British.
Apache	This tribe was composed of the Chiricahua, Jicarilla, Mescalero, San Carlos, White Mountain, and Kiowa-Apache tribes. They lived in the Southwest plains and spoke an Athapaskan dialect.
Arapaho	Speaking an Alogonquin dialect, the Arapaho lived in the Upper Platte River country and were closely allied with the Cheyenne.
Arikara	A war-like tribe which lived in earthen lodges along the Missouri River. They spoke a Caddoan dialect and were related to the Pawnee tribe.
Atsina	This tribe lived on or near the Milk and Saskatchewan Rivers in northern Montana and Alberta, Canada. They were also called the Gros Ventre of the Prairies as well as the White Clay People. They spoke an Algonquian dialect, were an offshoot of the Arapaho, and at times were allied with the Blackfoot Confederacy.

Bannock	A branch of the Northern Paiute tribe, these people dwelled in southeastern Idaho. They spoke a Uto-Aztecan dialect and were usually allied with the Snake River and Mountain Shoshone.
Bateau	A light boat with a flat bottom, tapered at both ends.
Big Horn Hot Springs	This famous spring is now called "Thermopolis" and is located in northern Wyoming on the Bighorn River. Its temperature ranges between 128 and 130 degrees Fahrenheit and it flows at three million gallons per day. As the heated water evaporates, it leaves large mounds of travertine deposits that resemble ice floes. Where the hot water enters the Bighorn River, temperatures vary from very hot to cold the farther you get from the flow. Today several commercial bathhouses and a state park are located at the spring.
Big Muddy River	Many Indians and early mountain men referred to the Missouri River as the "Big Muddy."
Blackfoot	The Algonquian-speaking Blackfoot Confederacy consisted of the Piegan, Blood and Northern Blackfeet or Siksika tribes. They controlled the upper reaches of the Missouri River, its tributaries, and the Saskatchewan River region of Alberta, Canada. They were friendly with the British but hostile to Americans and were constantly at war with the Crow.
Bois d' arc	This wood is also called Osage

orangewood. The Plains Indians favored it for bow-making. The tree has a white, sticky sap and is easily identified by its large green apples.

Calumet
The long, ornamental smoking pipe of the Plains Indians was usually made from a red stone quarried in Minnesota. The pipestone was named "Catlinite" after the painter of North American Indians, George Catlin.

Cayuse
A tribe that resided in the northwest and spoke a Penutian dialect. They were related to and allied with their neighbors, the Nez Perce. Like the Nez Perce, the Cayuse were excellent horse breeders.

Columbia Fur Company
This fur-trading company was founded and administered by Kenneth Mackenzie for trade in the Rocky Mountains. In 1828 the firm was taken over by John Jacob Astor's American Fur Company.

Comanche
Allied with the Kiowa, this tribe also spoke a Uto-Aztecan dialect and lived on the south plains. Excellent horsemen, they were very warlike.

Corps of Discovery
President Jefferson set forth the secret Lewis and Clark Expedition in 1803 and called the project "The Corps of Discovery." He led his enemies to believe that Lewis and Clark were sent to explore the Mississippi River. Instead they were to explore and map the new Louisiana Purchase and to find an overland route to the Pacific Ocean.

Coulee	A deep ravine or gulch.
Delaware	A northeastern tribe who spoke an Algonquian dialect. They scattered after their defeat by General Anthony Wayne in 1795. Many joined the Rocky Mountain fur trade companies as "free trappers."
Diggers	This was a derogatory term applied to the horseless, desert Shoshone tribes who dwelled in the area of Nevada and California. They spoke a Uto-Aztecan dialect.
Elk River	The Crow Indians called the Yellowstone the "Elk River."
Erarapi'o	The Crow name for the "Kicked-in-their-bellies," a branch of the Mountain Crow. They generally lived in the Wind River region of Wyoming.
Foofooraw	The mountain men used this term to refer to gaudy trade items desired by the Native American women.
French Fur Company	Founded in the Upper Missouri country in 1829, this company consisted of the French families known as Papin, Chenie, Cerr'es, Delaurier, Picotte, Guion, and Bonfort. The firm had assets of $16,000.
Gewgaws	A mountain man term for gaudy trade items preferred by Native American women. A gewgaw is usually an ornament.
Hidatsa	Relatives and most often allies of the Crow and Mandan. They spoke a Siouan dialect and lived near the Mandan in earthen Lodges on the

Missouri River in North Dakota. They were also called the Gros Ventre of the Missouri and Minitari (or Minetaree).

Horses River The Crow used this name to refer to the present day Pryor Creek.

Kinnikinnick Term used for Native American tobacco mixed with sumac leaves and the dried inner bark of red alder, dogwood, or red willow.

Latter-Day Saints These people were also referred to as Mormons. They lived in the Utah Territory. They kept good relations with most of the Indian tribes of Utah, Idaho and Wyoming.

Leaf-falling season Fall of the year.

Mackinaw boat A large, flat-bottomed boat with a stern rudder-sweep. Some had masts for sails and a superstructure for passengers.

Mandan A tribe of Siouan-speaking people who lived in earthen lodges on the Missouri River in North Dakota. They traded agricultural products to the Crow for horses, clothing, furs and robes.

Medicine Wheel Built by unknown, prehistoric people, the wheel lies prone in the northern portion of the Bighorn Mountains of Wyoming. The wheel has 28 spokes and is about 250 feet in diameter. Some Crow believed the wheel had mystical powers.

Missouri Fur Company Following on the heels of the Lewis and Clark Expedition, Manuel Lisa, William Morrison, and Pierre Menard founded the Missouri Fur Company in 1807. They built Fort Raymond (or Fort Manuel) at the mouth of the Bighorn River in order to trade with the Crow. Later they expanded and called the firm the St. Louis Missouri Fur Company. Lisa died in 1820 and the firm ceased operations in 1825.

Mohave
This tribe spoke a Yuman dialect and dwelled on the Colorado River area of Arizona, California and Nevada.

Mormons
Also known as Latter-Day Saints, these people settled and established the Utah Territory in the middle 1800s.

Muddy River
Another name for the Missouri River.

Nez Perce'
This Penutian-speaking tribe lived in Idaho, Oregon and Washington. They excelled in horse breeding and horse trading. They were credited with developing the Appaloosa horse and were allied with the Cayuse, who were also excellent horsemen. Nez Perce' in French means "pierced noses."

North West Company
Founded in 1784 to rival the Hudson's Bay Company, the British government forced the two firms to merge in 1821.

Obsidian
This is a black, hard lava glass that the Indians flaked or chipped to create arrow and spear points. It would not rust and tests have shown it to be sharper than steel points. Obsidian points penetrated animal flesh deeper than steel. The great Obsidian Cliff is located at the headwaters of the Yellowstone River in Yellowstone National Park.

Osage Orangewood	This wood is also known as *bois d' arc* and proved excellent for making bows. It was well used by the Plains Indians.
Parfleche	This is a Canuck-French word meaning "rawhide." Native Americans and mountain men used animal skins laced together to hold food, clothing, and personal effects. They folded the skins or hides like an envelope and many were elaborately decorated.
Pawnee	A Caddoan-speaking tribe, the Pawnee lived in the area of Kansas and Nebraska. They were housed in dome-shaped earthen lodges with an outer covering of grass and leaves.
Pecuni	The Crow used this name to refer to the Piegan tribe of the Blackfoot Confederacy.
Pemmican	Buffalo or other game meat cut into long, thin strips and dried. The hardened jerky is then pounded into powder and mixed with pulverized, fresh berries. Suet is poured over the mixture, which is then stored or sealed in parfleches or rawhide casings. The product could be traded as a commodity or kept as a nutritious food during the hard, cold winter.
Piegan	An Algonquin-speaking branch of the Blackfoot Confederacy. They lived in northwestern Montana and southern Alberta, Canada.
Pierced Nose	The French meaning of the name for the Nez Perce' tribe.

Plains Cree	A branch of the Kristinaux tribe who speak an Algonquian dialect. They dwelled in large areas of central Canada.
Pompey's Pillar	A stone tower located on the Yellowstone River approximately 25 miles northeast of Billings, Montana. William Clark named the tower in honor of Sacagawea's son, who was nicknamed "Pomp" This name meant "first born" in Shoshone.
Possibles	A mountain man term referring to personal effects.
Pine Leaf	The Crow name given to Woman Chief when she was captured from the Atsina at age 10. In 1856, Jim Beckwith documented her exploits in his book, *The Life and Adventures of James P. Beckwourth.*
Pox	A slang term referring to the dreaded smallpox disease.
Rocky Mountain Fur Company	Firm established in 1822 by General William H. Ashley. He made a fortune and sold out to his men, Smith, Jackson and Sublette. In 1830 they sold the company to Fitzpatrick, Bridger, Sublette, Fraeb and Gervais. The firm went out of business in 1834.
Seminole	This tribe originated from the Muskogean speaking Oconee of Georgia. They relocated to Florida about 1750. They were at war with the U. S. Army from 1817 to 1818 and from 1835 to 1842. Jim Beckwith fought in the Seminole War around 1838 and 1839.

Shining Mountains	Several tribes referred to the Rocky Mountains as the Shining Mountains.
Shoshone	A Uto-Aztecan-speaking tribe, the Shoshone were allied with the Bannock and at times with the Crow. They were also called the "Snake Indians" and various bands roamed from the Yellowstone National Park region, Wind River Valley, Green River and Bear River. They were usually friendly with the white trappers.
Shining Sun	This is the birth name given by the author to Woman Chief when she lived with her native tribe, the Atsina.
Snake Indians	Because sign language for Shoshone resembled the movement of a snake, they were referred to as the Snake Indians. The river that the main tribe lived on is still called the Snake River. They spoke a Uto-Aztecan dialect.
Snow-falling season	This refers to the winter season.
Sparrowhawk	This is the true name of the Crow Indians. The French name and English translation misinterpreted the name as "Crow."
Throwing bones	An Indian gambling game of tossing marked bones with a basket or with sticks.
White Clay People	The name the Atsina called themselves. They were also known as the Gros Ventres of the Prairies.
Woman Chief	The adult war chief name given to Pine Leaf as reported by Edwin T. Denig in his 1856 book, *Five Indian Tribes of the Upper Missouri*.

Printed in the United States
65441LVS00004B/220-270

9 781425 981341